Alfred John Church, Ruth Putnam

The Count of the Saxon Shore, or, The Villa in Vectis

A Tale of the Departure of the Romans from Britain

Alfred John Church, Ruth Putnam

The Count of the Saxon Shore, or, The Villa in Vectis
A Tale of the Departure of the Romans from Britain

ISBN/EAN: 9783744782166

Printed in Europe, USA, Canada, Australia, Japan

Cover: Foto ©Andreas Hilbeck / pixelio.de

More available books at **www.hansebooks.com**

The COUNT of the SAXON SHORE

or

The Villa in VECTIS

A TALE OF THE DEPARTURE OF THE ROMANS FROM BRITAIN

BY THE

REV. ALFRED J. CHURCH, M.A.

Author of "Stories from Homer"

WITH THE COLLABORATION OF
RUTH PUTNAM

Fifth Thousand

LONDON
SEELEY, SERVICE & CO. LIMITED
38 GREAT RUSSELL STREET

PREFACE.

"COUNT OF THE SAXON SHORE" was a title bestowed by Maximian (colleague of Diocletian in the Empire from 286 to 305 A.D.) on the officer whose task it was to protect the coasts of Britain and Gaul from the attacks of the Saxon pirates. It appears to have existed down to the abandonment of Britain by the Romans.

So little is known from history about the last years of the Roman occupation that the writer of fiction has almost a free hand. In this story a novel, but, it is hoped, not an improbable, view is taken of an important event—the withdrawal of the legions. This is commonly assigned to the year 410, when the Emperor Honorius formally withdrew the Imperial protection from Britain. But the usurper Constantine had actually removed the British army two years before; and, as he was busied with the conquest of Gaul and Spain for a considerable time after, it is not likely that they were ever sent back.

A. J. C.
R. P.

CONTENTS.

CONTENTS.

LIST OF ILLUSTRATIONS.

THE COUNT OF THE SAXON SHORE.

CHAPTER I.

A BRITISH CÆSAR.

"Hail! Cæsar Emperor, the starving salute thee!"[1] and the speaker made a military salute to a silver coin, evidently brand-new from the mint (which did not seem, by the way, to turn out very good work), and bearing the superscription, "Gratianus Cæsar Imperator Felicissimus." He was a soldier of middle age, whose jovial face did not show any sign of the fate which he professed to have so narrowly escaped, and formed one of a group which was lounging about the *Quæstorium*, or, as we may put it, the paymaster's office of the camp at the head of the Great Harbour.[2]

---

[1] A reference to the well-known salutation of the gladiators as they passed the Emperor in his seat at the Public Games. "Ave Cæsar Imperator! Morituri te salutant." *Hail! Cæsar Emperor, the doomed to death salute thee.*

[2] Now known all over the world as Portsmouth Harbour.

A very curious medley of nationalities was that group. There were Gauls; there were Germans from the Rhine bank, some of them of the pure Teuton type, with fair complexions, bright blue eyes, and reddish golden hair, and remarkably tall of stature, others showing an admixture of the Celtic blood of their Gallic neighbours in their dark hair and hazel eyes; there were swarthy Spaniards, fierce-looking men from the Eastern Adriatic, showing some signs of Greek parentage in their regular features and graceful figures; there were two or three who seemed to have an admixture of Asian or even African blood in them; it might be said, in fact, there were representatives of every province of the Empire, Italy only excepted. They had been just receiving their pay, long in arrear, and now considerably short of the proper amount, and containing not a few coins which the receivers seemed to think of doubtful value.

"Let me look at his Imperial Majesty," said another speaker; and he scanned the features of the new Cæsar—features never very dignified, and certainly not flattered by the rude coinage—with something like contempt. "Well, he does not look exactly as a Cæsar should; but what does it matter? This will go down with Rufus at the wine-shop and Priscus the sausage-seller, as well as the head of the great Augustus himself."

"Ah!" said a third speaker, picking out from

a handful of silver a coin which bore the head of Theodosius, "this was an Emperor worth fighting under. I made my first campaign with him against Maximus, another British Cæsar, by the way; and he was every inch a soldier. If his son were like him [1] things would be smoother than they are."

"Do you think," said the second speaker, after first throwing a cautious glance to see whether any officer of rank was in hearing—"do you think we have made a change for the better from Marcus? [2] He at all events used to be more liberal with his money than his present majesty. You remember he gave us ten silver pieces each. Now we don't even get our proper pay."

"Marcus, my dear fellow," said the other speaker, "had a full military chest to draw upon, and it was not difficult to be generous. Gratianus has to squeeze every denarius out of the citizens. I heard them say, when the money came into the camp yesterday, that it was a loan from the Londinium merchants. I wonder what interest they will get, and when they will see the principal again."

"Hang the fat rascals!" said the other. "Why

---

[1] Honorius and Arcadius, who ruled over the Western and Eastern Empires respectively, were the weak sons of the vigorous Theodosius.

[2] Marcus was the first of three usurpers successively saluted Emperor by the legions of Britain.

should they sleep soft, and eat and drink the best of everything, while we poor soldiers, who keep them and their money-bags safe, have to go bare and hungry ? "

" Come, come, comrades," interrupted the first soldier who had spoken; " no more grumbling, or some of us will find the centurion after us with his vine-sticks."

The group broke up, most of them making the best of their way to spend some of their unaccustomed riches at the wine-shop, a place from which they had lately kept an enforced absence. Three or four of the number, however, who seemed, from a sign that passed between them, to have some secret understanding, remained in close conversation—a conversation which they carried on in undertones, and which they adjourned to one of the tents to finish without risk of being disturbed or overheard.

The camp in which our story opens was a square enclosure, measuring some five hundred yards each way, and surrounded by a massive wall, not less than four feet in thickness, in the construction of which stone, brick, and tile had, in Roman fashion, been used together. The defences were completed by strong towers of a rounded shape, which had been erected at frequent intervals. The camp had, as usual, its four gates. That which opened upon the sea—for the sea washed the southern front—was famous in military tradition as the gate by which the second legion had embarked to take part in the Jewish War and the famous siege of Jerusalem. Vespasian, who had begun in Britain the great career which ended in the throne, had experienced its valour and discipline in more than one campaign,[1] and had paid it the high compliment of making a special request for its services when he was appointed to conduct what threatened to be a formidable war. This glorious recollection was proudly cherished in the camp, though more than three centuries had passed, changing as they went the aspect of the camp, till it looked at least as much like a town as a military post. The troops were housed in huts stoutly built of timber, which a visitor would have found comfortably furnished by a long succession of occupants. The quarters of the tribune and higher centurions were commodious dwellings of brick; and the headquarters of the legate, or commanding officer, with its handsome chambers, its baths, and tesselated pavements, might well have been a mansion at Rome. There was a street of regular shape, in which provisions, clothes, and even ornaments could

---

[1] Vespasian, appointed by Claudius in A.D. 52 to the command of the second legion, had made extensive conquests in Britain adding, among other places, the Isle of Wight (Vectis) to the Empire.

be bought.   Roman discipline, though somewhat relaxed, did not indeed permit the dealers to remain within the fortifications at night, but the shops were tenanted by day, and did a thriving business, not only with the soldiers, but with the Britons of the neighbourhood, who found the camp a convenient resort, where they could market to advantage, besides gossiping to their hearts' content.   The relations between the soldiers and their native neighbours were indeed friendly in the extreme.   The legion had had its headquarters in the camp of the Great Harbour for many generations, though it had occasionally gone on foreign service.   Lately, too, the policy which had recruited the British legion with soldiers from the Continent, had been relaxed, partly from carelessness, partly because it was necessary to fill up the ranks as could best be done, and there was but little choice of men.   Thus service became very much an inheritance.   The soldiers married British women, and their children, growing up, became soldiers in turn.   Many recruits still came from Gaul, Spain, and the mouth of the Rhine, and elsewhere, but quite as many of the troops were by this time, in part or in whole, British.

Another change which the three centuries and a half since Vespasian's time had brought about was in religion.   The temple of Mars, which had stood near the headquarters, and where the legate had been accustomed to take the auspices,[1] was now a Christian Church, duly served by a priest of British birth.

About a couple of hours later in the day a shout of " The Emperor! the Emperor!" was raised in the camp, and the soldiers, flocking out from the mess-tents in which most of them were sitting, lined in a dense throng the avenue which led from the chief gate to headquarters.

Gratianus, who was followed by a few officers of superior rank and a small escort of cavalry, rode slowly between the lines of soldiers. His reception was not as hearty as he had expected to find. He had, as the soldiers had hinted, made vast exertions to raise a sum of money in Londinium—then, as now, the wealthiest municipality in the island. Himself a native of the place, and connected with some of its richest citizens, he had probably got together more than any one else would have done in like circumstances. But all his persuasions and promises, even his offer of twenty per cent. interest, had not been able to extract from the Londinium burghers the full sum that was required ; and the soldiers, who the day before would have loudly proclaimed that they would be thankful for the smallest instalment, were now almost furious because they had not been paid in full. A few shouts of " Hail, Cæsar ! Hail,

---

[1] The observation of omens, or signs, supposed to indicate the future, was one of the duties of a commanding officer.

Gratianus! Hail, Britannicus!" greeted him on the road to his quarters; but these came from the front lines only, and chiefly from the centurions and deputy-centurions, while the great body of the soldiers maintained an ominous silence, sometimes broken by a sullen murmur.

Gratianus was not a man fitted to deal with sudden emergencies. He was rash and he was ambitious, but he wanted steadfast courage, and he was hampered by scruples of which an usurper must rid himself at once if he hopes to keep himself safe in his seat. He might have appealed frankly to the soldiers—asked them what it was they complained of, and taken them frankly into his confidence; or he might have overawed them by an example of severity, fixing on some single act of insubordination or insolence, and sending the offender to instant execution. He was not bold enough for either course, and the opportunity passed, as quickly as opportunities do in such times, hopelessly out of his reach.

The temper of the soldiers grew more excited and dangerous as the day went on. For many weeks past want of money had kept them sober against their will, and now that the long-expected pay-day had come they crowded the wine-shops inside and outside the camp, and drank almost as wildly as an Australian shepherd when he comes down to the town after a six months' solitude. As anything can set highly combustible materials on fire, so the most trivial and meaningless incident will turn a tipsy mob into a crowd of bloodthirsty madmen. Just before sunset a messenger entered the camp bringing a despatch from one of the outlying forts. One of those prodigious lies which seem always ready to start into existence when they are wanted for mischief at once ran like wild-fire through the camp. Gratianus was bringing together troops from other parts of the province, and was going to disarm and decimate the garrison of the Great Camp. The unfortunate messenger was seized before he could make his way to headquarters, seriously injured, and robbed of the despatch which he was carrying. Some of the centurions ventured to interfere and endeavour to put down the tumult. Two or three who were popular with the men were good-humouredly disarmed; others, who were thought too rigorous in discipline, were roughly handled and thrown into the military prison ; one, who had earned for himself the nick-name of "Old Hand me the other,"[1] was killed on the spot. The furious crowd then rushed to headquarters, where Gratianus was entertaining

---

[1] When one of the vine-sticks used in administering corporal punishment to the Roman soldiers was broken on the culprit's back, he would at once call for another. A milder disciplinarian would probably consider that when the stick was broken the punishment might end.

a company of officers of high rank, and clamoured that they must see the Emperor.   He came out and mounted the hustings, which stood near the front of the buildings, and from which it was usual to address gatherings of the soldiers.

For a moment the men, not altogether lost to the sense of discipline, were hushed into silence and order by the sight of the Emperor as he stood on the platform in his Imperial purple, his figure thrown into bold relief by the torches which his attendants held behind him.

"What do you want, my children?" he said; but there was a tremble in his voice which put fresh courage into the failing hearts of the mutineers.

"Give us our pay, give us our arrears!" answered a soldier in one of the back rows, emboldened to speak by finding himself out of sight.

The cry was taken up by the whole multitude. "Our pay!   Our pay!" was shouted from thousands of throats.

Gratianus stood perplexed and irresolute, visibly cowering before the storm.   At this moment one of the tribunes stepped forward and whispered in his ear.   What he said was this : "Say to them, ' Follow me, and I will give you all you ask and more.'"

It was a happy suggestion, one of the vague promises that commit to nothing, and if the unlucky usurper could have given it with confidence, with an air that gave it a meaning, he might have been saved, at least for a time. But his nerve, his presence of mind was hopelessly lost. " Follow me—where ? Whither am I to lead them ? " he asked, in a hurried, agitated whisper.

His adviser shrugged his shoulders and was silent. He saw that he was not comprehended.

Gratianus continued to stand silent and irresolute, with his helpless, despairing gaze fixed upon the crowd. Then came a great surging movement from the back of the crowd, and the front ranks were almost forced up the steps of the platform. The unlucky prince turned as if to flee. The movement sealed his fate. A stone hurled from the back of the crowd struck him on the side of the face. Half stunned by the blow, he leaned against one of the attendants, and the blood could be seen pouring down his face, pale with terror, and looking ghastly in the flaming torchlight. The next moment the attendant flung down his torch and fled—an example followed by all his companions. Then all was in darkness ; and it only wanted darkness to make a score of hands busy in the deed of blood.

As Gratianus lay prostrate on the ground the first blow was aimed by a brother of his predecessor, Marcus, who had been quietly waiting for an opportunity of vengeance. In another minute he had ceased to live. His head was severed from the body and fixed on the top of a pike. One of the murderers seized a smouldering torch, and, blowing it into flame, held it up while another exhibited the bleeding head, and cried, " The tyrant has his deserts ! " But by this time the mad rage of the crowd had subsided. The horror of the deed had sobered them. Many began to remember little acts of kindness which the murdered man had done them, and the feeling of wrong was lost in a revulsion of pity. In a few moments more the crowd was scattered. Silent and remorseful the men went to their quarters, and the camp was quiet again. But another British Cæsar had gone the way of a long line of unlucky predecessors.

CHAPTER II.

AN ELECTION.

THE camp next day was covered with gloom. The soldiers moved silent and with downcast faces along the avenues, or discharged in a mechanical way their routine duties. The guards were turned out, the sentries relieved, and the general order of service maintained without any action on the part of the officers—at least of those who held superior rank. These remained in the seclusion of their tents ; and it may be said that those who were conscious of being popular were almost as much alarmed as those who knew that they were disliked. If the latter dreaded the vengeance of those whom they had offended, the others were scarcely less alarmed by the possibility of being elected to the perilous dignity which had just proved fatal to Gratianus. The country people, whose presence generally gave an air of cheerfulness and activity to the camp, were too much alarmed to come. The trading booths inside the gates were empty, and only a very few stalls were occupied in the market, which was held every day outside them.

The funeral of the late prince was celebrated with some pomp. The soldiers attended it in crowds, and manifested their grief, and, it would seem, their remorse, by groans and tears. They were ready even to give proofs of their repentance by the summary execution of those who had taken an active part in the bloody deed. But here, one of the centurions, whose cheerful, genial manners made him an unfailing favourite with the men, had the courage to check them. "No, my men," said he; "we were all mad last night, and we must all take the blame."

Two days passed without any incident of importance. On the third the question of a successor began to be discussed. One of the other garrisons might be beforehand with them, and they would have either to accept a chief who would owe his best favours to others, or risk their lives in an unprofitable struggle with him. In the afternoon a general assembly of the troops was held, the officers still holding aloof, though some of them mixed, *incognito*, so to speak, in the crowd.

Of course, the first difficulty was to find any one who would take the lead. At last the genial centurion, who has been mentioned above as a well-established favourite with the soldiers, was pushed to the front. His speech was short and sensible. "Comrades," he said, "I doubt whether what I have to say will please you ; but I shall say it all the same. You know that I always speak my mind. We have not done very well in the new ways. Let us try the old. I propose that we take the oath to Honorius Augustus."

A deep murmur of discontent ran through the assembly, and showed that the speaker had pre-sumed at least as far as was safe on his popularity with the troops.

"Does Decius," cried a burly German from the crowd—Decius was the name of the centurion—"does Decius recommend that we should trust to the mercy of Honorius ? Very good, perhaps, for him-self; for the giver of such advice could scarcely fail of a reward; but for us it means decimation [1] at the least."

A shout of applause showed that the speaker had expressed the feelings of his audience.

"I propose that we all take the oath to Decius himself!" said a Batavian; "he is a brave man and an honest, and what do we want more ? "

The good Decius had heard undismayed the angry

---

[1] " Decimation " was a common military punishment in cases of mutiny or bad behaviour on the field of battle. Every tenth man, taken by lot, was put to death.

disapproval which his loyal proposal had called forth; but the mention of his name as a possible candidate for the throne overwhelmed him with terror. His jovial face grew pale as death; the sweat stood in large drops upon his forehead; he trembled as he had never trembled in the face of an enemy.

"Comrades," he stammered, "what have I done that you should treat me thus? If I have offended or injured you, kill me, but not this."

More than half possessed by a spirit of mischief, the assembly answered this piteous appeal by continuous shouts of "Long live the Emperor Decius!"

The good man grew desperate. He drew his sword from the scabbard, and pointed it at his own heart. "At least," he cried, "you can't forbid me this escape."

The bystanders wrested the weapon from him; but the joke had gone far enough, and the man was too genuinely popular for the soldiers to allow him to be tormented beyond endurance. A voice from the crowd shouted, "Long live the Centurion Decius!" to which another answered, "Long live Decius the subject!" and the worthy man felt that the danger was over.

A number of candidates, most of whom were probably as little desirous of the honour as Decius, were now proposed in succession.

"I name the Tribune Manilius," said one of the soldiers.

The name was received with a shout of laughter.

"Let him learn first to be Emperor at home!" cried a voice from the back of the assembly, a sally which had considerable success, as his wife was a well-known termagant, and his two sons the most frequent inmates of the military prison.

"I name the Centurion Pisinna."

"Very good, if he does not pledge the purple," for Pisinna was notoriously impecunious.

"I name the Tribune Cetronius."

"Very good as Emperor of the baggage-guard." Cetronius had, to say the least, no high reputation for personal courage, and was supposed to prefer the least exposed parts on the field.

A number of other names were mentioned only to be dismissed with more or less contumely. Tired of this sport—for it really was nothing more—the crowd cried out for a speech from a well-known orator of the camp, whose fluency, not unmixed with shrewd-ness and humour, had gained him a considerable reputation among his comrades.

"Comrades," he began, "if you have not yet found a candidate worthy of your suffrages, it is not because such do not exist among you. Can it be believed that Britain is less worthy to produce the Emperor than Gaul, or Spain, or Thrace, or even the effeminate

Syria ? Was it not from Britain that there came forth the greatest of the successors of Augustus, the Second Romulus, Flavius Aurelius Constantinus ? " [1]

The orator was not permitted to proceed any further. The name Constantinus ran like an electric shock through the whole assembly, and a thousand voices took up the cry, " Long live Constantinus, Emperor Augustus ! " while all eyes were turned to one of the back rows of the meeting, where a soldier who happened to bear that name was standing. Some of his comrades caught him by the arm, hurried him to the front, and from thence on to the hustings. He was greeted with a perfect uproar of applause, partly, of course, ironical, but partly the expression of a genuine feeling that the right man had been found, and found by some sort of Divine assistance. The soldiers were, as has been said, a strange medley of men, scarcely able to understand each other, and alike only in being savage, ignorant, and superstitious. They had been unlucky in choosing for themselves, and now it might be well to have the choice made for them. And at least the new man had a name which all of them knew and reverenced, as far as they reverenced anything.

---

[1] It would seem that the myth which made the Empress Helena, the mother of Constantine, into a British princess, had already grown up. She was, in fact, the daughter of a **tavern-keeper**, and in no way connected with Britain.

Constantine elected Emperor.

Whether he had anything but a name might have seemed perhaps somewhat doubtful. He had reached middle age, for he had two sons already grown up, but had never risen above the rank of a private soldier. It might be said, perhaps, that he had shown some ability in thus avoiding promotion—not always a desirable thing in troublous times; but there was the fact that he was nearly fifty years of age, and was not even a deputy-centurion. On the other hand, he was a respectable man, ignorant indeed, for, like most of his comrades, he could neither read nor write, but with a certain practical shrewdness, so good-humoured that he had never made an enemy, known to be remarkably brave, a great athlete in his youth, and still of a strength beyond the average.

His sudden and strange elevation did not seem to throw him in the least off his balance. He had been perfectly content to go without promotion, and now he seemed equally content to receive the highest promotion of all. He stood calmly facing the excited mob, as unmoved as if he had been a private soldier on the parade ground. A slight flush, indeed, might have been seen to mount to his face when the cloak of imperial purple was thrown over his shoulders, and the peaked diadem put upon his head. He must have been less than man not to have felt some thrill either of fear or pride at the touch of what had brought two of his comrades to their graves within the space of less than half a year ; but he showed no other sign of emotion.

The officers, seeing the turn things had taken, had now come to the front, and the senior tribune, taking the new Emperor by the hand, led him to the edge of the hustings, and said, " Comrades, I present to you Aurelius Constantinus, chosen by the providence of God and the choice of the army to be Emperor of Britain and the West. The Blessed and Undivided Trinity order it for the best." A ringing shout of approval went up in response. The tribunes then took the oath of allegiance to the new Emperor in person. These again administered it to the centurions, and the centurions swore in great batches of the soldiers. The new-made prince meanwhile stood unmoved, it might almost be said insensible, so strange was his composure in the face of his sudden elevation. All that he said—the result, it seemed, of a whisper from one of his sons—were a few words, which, however, had all the success of a most eloquent oration.

" Comrades, I promise you a donative [1] within the space of a month."

The assembly broke up in great good-humour, and the newly-made Emperor, attended by the officers, went to take possession of headquarters.

---

[1] A *donative* was a distribution of money made to the soldiers on such occasions as the accession of an Emperor.

CHAPTER III.

A PRIZE.

IT was a bright morning some three weeks after the occurrences related in the last chapter, when a squadron of four Roman galleys swept round the point which is now known as the South Foreland. The leader of the four, all of which, indeed, lay so close together as to be within easy hailing distance, bore on its mainmast the *Labarum*, or Imperial standard, showing on a ground of purple a cross, a crown, and the sacred initials, all wrought in gold. It was the flagship, so to speak, of the great Count himself, one of the most important lieutenants of the Empire, whose task it was to guard the shores of Britain and Northern Gaul from the pirate swarms that issued from the harbours of the North Sea and the Baltic. The Count himself was on board, coming south from his villa on the eastern shore—for the stations of which he had the charge extended as far as the Wash—to his winter residence in the sunny island of Vectis.

The Count was a tall man of middle age, and wore over his tunic a military cloak reaching to the hips, and clasped at the neck with a handsome device in gold, representing a hunting-dog with his teeth fixed in a stag. His head was covered with a broad-brimmed hat of felt. The only weapon that he carried was a short sword, which, with its plain hilt and leather scabbard, was evidently meant for use rather than show. His whole appearance and bearing, indeed, were those of a man of action and energy. His eyes were bright and piercing; his nose showed, strongly pronounced, the curve which has always been associated with the ability to command; the contour of his chin and lips, as far as could be seen through a short curling beard and moustache, worn as a prudent defence against the climate, betokened firmness. Still, the expression of the face was not unkindly. As a great writer says of one whom Britain had had good reason in earlier days both to fear and to love, "one would easily believe him to be a good man, and willingly believe him to be great."

At the time when our story opens he was standing in conversation with the helmsman, a weather-beaten old sailor, whose dark Southern complexion had been deepened by the sun and winds of more than fifty years of service into an almost African hue.

"The wind will hardly serve us as well as it has," said the Count, as his practised eye, familiar with every yard of the coast, perceived that they were well abreast of the extreme southern point of the coast.

" No, my lord," said the old man, "we shall have to take as long a tack as we can to the south. There is a deal of west in the wind—more, I think, than there was an hour since. Castor and Pollux—I beg your lordship's pardon, the blessed Saints—defend us from anything like a westerly gale."

"Ah! old croaker," replied the Count, with a laugh, " I verily believe that you will be half disappointed if we get to our journey's end without some mishap.

" Good words, good words, my lord," said the old man, hastily crossing himself, while he muttered something, which, if it could have been overheard, would have been scarcely suitable to that act of devotion. " Heaven bring us safe to our journey's end ! Of course it is your lordship's business to give orders, and ours to go to the bottom, if it is to be so. But I must say, saving your presence, that it is against all rules of a sailor's craft as I have known it, man and boy, for nigh upon threescore years, to be at sea near about a month after the autumn equinox.

> ' Never let your keel be wet,
> When the Pleiades have set ;
> Never let your keel be dry,
> When the Crown is in the sky.'

That is what my father used to say, and his fathers before him, for I do not know how many generations, for we have always followed the sea."

"Very well for them, perhaps," said the Count, " in the days when a man would almost as soon go into a lion's den as venture out of sight of land. But the world is too busy to let us waste half our year on shore."

" Yes, yes, I know all about that," answered the old man, who was privileged to have the last word even with so great a personage as the Count ; " but there is a proverb, ' Much haste, little speed,' and I have always found it quite as true by sea as by land."

Meanwhile the proper signals had been given to the rest of the squadron, and the whole four were now heading south, with a point or two to the west, the *Panther*—for that was the name of the flagship— still slightly leading the way, with her consorts in close company.   In this order they made about twelve miles, the wind freshening somewhat as they drew further away from the British shore, and, being nearly aft, carrying them briskly along.

" Fine sailing, fine sailing," said the old helms- man, drawn almost in spite of himself into an ex- clamation of delight, as the *Panther*, rushing through the water with an almost even keel, began to widen the gap between herself and her nearest follower.

The short waves, which just broke in sparkling foam, the brilliant sunshine, almost bringing back summer with its noonday heat, and the sea with a blue which recalled, though but faintly, the deep tint of his native Mediterranean, combined to gladden the old man's soul. " But we need not put about now," he said to himself. " If this wind holds we shall fetch Lemanis [1] without requiring to tack."

He was about to give the necessary orders to trim the sails, when he was stopped by a shout from the look-out man at the bow, "A sail on the starboard side !" Just within the range of a keen sight, in the south-western horizon, the sunlight fell on what was evidently a sail. But the distance was too great to let even the keenest sight distinguish what kind of craft it might be, or which way it was moving. The Count, who had gone below for his mid-day meal, was of course informed of the news. He came at once upon deck, and lost no time in making up his mind.

" If she is an enemy," he said to the old helmsman, " she will be eastward bound; though I never knew a pirate keep the sea quite so late in the year. If she is a friend she will probably be sailing westward, or even coming our way—but it does not matter which. If she has anything to tell us, we

---

[1] Lymne, in Kent, now some miles inward, on the edge of Romney Marsh.

shall be sure to hear it sooner or later. But it will never do to let a pirate escape if we can help it. Any one who is out so late as the middle of October must have had good reason for stopping, and can hardly fail to be worth catching. Quintus, put her right before the wind, and clap on every inch of canvas."

The course of the squadron was now changed to nearly due south-east. All eyes, of course, were bent on the strange craft, and before an hour had passed it was evident that the Count had been right in his guess. There were four ships; they were long and low in the water, of the build which was only too well known along the coasts of Gaul and Britain, where no river or creek, if it gave as much as three or four feet of water, was safe from their attack. In short, they were Saxon pirates, and were now moving eastward with all the speed that sails and oars could give them. The question that every one on board the *Panther* was putting to himself with intense interest was, "Shall we be able to intercept them?" For the present the Count's ship had the advantage of speed, thanks to the wind abaft the beam. But a stern chase would be useless. On equal terms the pirates were at least as quick as their pursuers. The light, too, of the autumn day would soon fail, and with the light every chance of success would be gone.

For a time it seemed as if the escape of the pirate was certain. " Curse the scoundrels ! " cried the Count, as he paced impatiently up and down the after deck. " If it would only come on to blow in real earnest we should have them. Anyhow, I would sooner that we should all founder together than that they should get off scot free."

The *Panther*, which had left her consorts about a mile in the rear, was now near enough for her crew to see distinctly the outlines of the pirate ships, to mark the glitter of the shields that were ranged along the gunwales, and to catch the rhythmic rise and fall of the long sweeping oars. The Saxons were evidently straining every nerve to make good their escape, and it seemed scarcely possible that they could fail. Then came a turn of fortune—the very thing, in fact, that the Count had prayed for. For a time—only a very few moments—the wind freshened to something like the force of a gale. The masts of the *Panther* were strained to the utmost of their strength ; they groaned and bent like whips under the sudden pressure on the canvas, but the seasoned timber stood the sudden call upon it bravely. How the Count blessed himself that he had never passed over a piece of bad workmanship or bad material ! The good ship took a wild plunge forward, but nothing gave way. But the last of the four pirates was not so fortunate. She had one tall mast, carrying a fore-and-aft sail, so large as to be quite out of proportion to her size. The wind struck her nearly sideways, and she heeled over till her keel could almost be seen. For a moment it was doubtful whether she would not capsize. Then the mast gave. The vessel righted at once, but only to lie utterly helpless on the water, with all her starboard oars hopelessly entangled with the canvas and rigging. What the Count would have done had his ship been entirely in hand it is difficult to say. No speedier or more effective way of dealing with the enemy than running her down could have been practised. The *Panther* had three or four times the tonnage of her adversary, whose lightness and low bulwarks made her easily accessible to this kind of attack. Nor would the pirates have a chance of showing the desperate valour which the Roman boarding-parties had learnt to respect and almost to fear. The only argument on the other side would have been that prisoners and booty would probably be lost. But, as a matter of fact, the Count had no opportunity of weighing the *pros* and *cons* in the matter. The *Panther*, driving as she was straight before the wind, was practically unmanageable. She struck the pirate craft with a tremendous crash amidships, and cut her almost literally in half. One blow, and one only, did the pirates strike at their conquerors. When escape had become manifestly

The Panther and the Saxon Pirate.

impossible by the fall of the mast, the Saxon warriors had dropped their oars, and seizing their bows had discharged a volley of arrows against the Roman ship. The hurry and confusion of the moment did not favour accurate aim, and most of the missiles flew wide of the mark; but one seemed to have been destined to fulfil the helmsman's expectations of evil to come. It struck the old man on the left side, inflicting a fatal wound. In the first confusion of the shock the incident was not noticed, for the brave fellow stuck gallantly to the tiller, propping himself up against it while he kept the *Panther* steadily before the wind. In fact, loss of blood had brought him nearly to his end before it was even known that he had been wounded. Then, in a moment, the Count was at his side.

" Carry him to my own cabin," he said.

The old man raised his hand in a gesture that seemed to refuse the service which half a dozen stout sailors were at once ready to render him. " Nay," said he, " it is idle; this arrow has sped me. But let me die here, where I can see the waves and the sky. I have known them, man and boy, threescore years—aye, and more, for my father would take me on his ship when I was a tiny chap of three feet high. Nay, no cabin for me; 'tis almost as bad as dying in one's bed."

His voice grew feeble. The Count stopped, and

asked whether there was anything that he could do for him.

"Nay," said the old man, "nothing; I have neither chick nor child. 'Tis all as well as I could have wished. But mark, my lord, I was right about sailing in October. Any one that knows the sea would be sure that trouble must come of it."

The next moment he was past speaking or hearing.

It was his privilege, we must remember, to have the last word.

The *Panther* meanwhile had been brought to the wind. Her consorts, too, had come up, and a search was made for any survivors of the encounter that might be still afloat. Some had been killed outright by the concussion; others had been so hurt that they could make no effort to save themselves. They would not, however, have made it if they could. Those that had escaped uninjured evidently preferred drowning to a Roman prison. With grim resolution they straightened their arms to their sides and went down. Only two survivors were picked up. These, evidently twins from their close resemblance to each other, were found clinging to a fragment of timber. One had been grievously hurt, the other had not suffered any injury.

The wounded man, who had received an almost fatal blow upon the head, had lost the power to move, and was holding on to life more than half unconsciously ; and his brother, moved by that passionate love so often found between twins, had sacrificed himself—that is, the honour which he counted dearer than life—to save him. Had he had only himself to think of, he would have been the first to go down a free man to the bottom of the sea ; but his brother was almost helpless, and he could not leave him.

When it was evident that all further search would be useless, the squadron set their sails for Lemanis, which, thanks to a further change in the wind to the northward, they were able to reach before midnight.

CHAPTER IV.

THE VILLA IN THE ISLAND.

Count ÆLIUS was a man of the best Roman type, a man of "primitive virtue," as the classical writers would have put it, though this virtue had been softened, refined, and purified by civilizing and instructing influences, of which the old Roman heroes —the Fabiuses, the Catos, the Scipios—had known nothing. In the antiquity of his lineage there was scarcely a man in the Empire who could pretend to compare with him. For the most part, the old houses from which had come the Consuls and Dictators of the Republic had died out. The old nobility had gone, and the new nobility had followed it. The great name of Fabius, saved by an accident from extinction, when its three hundred gallant sons, each of them "fit to command an army," perished in one day by the craft of the Etruscan foe, had passed away. There was no living representative of the conqueror of Carthage, or of the conqueror of Corinth. Even the *parvenus* of the Empire had in their turn disappeared. The generals and senators, both of the old Rome and of the new,[1] bore names which would have sounded strange and barbarous to Cicero or even to Tacitus. An Ælius then, one who claimed to trace his descent to a time even earlier than the legendary age, to a race which was domiciled in Italy long before even Æneas had brought thither the gods of Troy, was an almost singular phenomenon in a generation of new men. And nothing less than this was the pedigree claimed by the Ælii. Their remotest ancestor—the Count never could hear an allusion to it without a smile— was the famous cannibal king who ruled over the Lasetrygones, a tribe of Western Italy,[2] and from whose jaws the prudent Ulysses so narrowly escaped. The pride of ancient descent is not particular as to the character of a progenitor, so he be suffi- ciently remote; and one branch of the Ælii had always delighted to recall by their surname their connection with this man-eating hero. But the race had not lacked glories of its own in historical times. They had had soldiers, statesmen, and men of letters among them. One of them had been made immortal by the friendship of Horace. Another, an adopted

---

[1] Constantinople.

[2] His capital is said to have been near the ancient Caieta and modern Gaieta.

son, it was true, better known by the famous name of Sejanus, had nearly made himself master of the throne of the Cæsars. About a hundred years later this crowning glory of human ambition had fallen to it in the person of Hadrian, third in the list of the " five good Emperors ";[1] though indeed there were purists in the matter of genealogy who stoutly denied that this great soldier and scholar had any of the real Ælian blood in him.

The Count's father had held civil office at Carthage, and the young Ælius had there, for a short time, been a pupil of Aurelius Augustinus, then known as an eloquent teacher of rhetoric, afterwards to become the most famous doctor of the Western Church. But his bent was not for the profession of the law, and his father, though disappointed at his preference for a soldier's career, would not stand in his way. His first experience of warfare was gained on a day of terrible disaster. His father's influence had secured him a position which seemed in every way desirable. He was attached to the staff of Trajanus, a general of division in the army of the Emperor Valens. By great exertions, travelling night and day, at the hottest period of the year, the

[1] The " five " are, Nerva, Trajan, Hadrian, Antoninus Pius, and Marcus Aurelius, whose united reigns extended from 97 to 180 A.D.—a period of peace and prosperity such as Rome never enjoyed again.

young Ælius contrived to report himself to his commander on the eve of the great battle of Adrianople. He had borne himself with admirable courage and self-possession during that terrible day, more disastrous to the Roman arms than even Cannæ itself. He had helped to carry the wounded Emperor to a cottage near the field of battle, and had barely escaped with his life, cutting his way with desperate resolution through the enemy, when this place of refuge was surrounded and burnt by the barbarians. After this unfortunate beginning he betook himself for a time to the employments of peace, obtaining an office under Government at Milan, where he renewed his acquaintance with his old teacher, Augustine. Then another opening, in what was still his favourite profession, presented itself. The young soldier's gallant conduct on the disastrous day of Adrianople had not been forgotten by some who had witnessed it, and when Stilicho, then the rising general of the Empire, was looking about for officers to fill posts upon his staff, the name of Ælius was mentioned to him. Under Stilicho he served with much distinction, and it was on Stilicho's recommendation that he was appointed to the post which, when our story opens, he had held for nearly twenty years.

His position during this period had been one of singular difficulty. The tie between the Empire and Britain was very loose. More than once during

Ælius' tenure of office it had seemed to be broken altogether. Pretender after pretender had risen against the central power, and had declared his province independent, and himself an Emperor. The Count of the Saxon Shore had contrived to keep himself neutral, so to speak, during these troubles. His own office, that of defending the eastern and southern shores of the island against the attacks of the Saxon pirates, he had filled with remarkable vigilance and skill. And the usurpers had been content to leave him undisturbed. His sailors were profoundly attached to him, and any attempt to interfere with him would have thrown a considerable weight into the opposite scale. And he and his work were necessary. Whether Britain was subject to Rome or independent of it, it was equally important that its coasts should not be harried by pirates. If Ælius would provide for this—and he did provide for it, with an almost unvarying success— he might be left alone, and not required to give in his allegiance to the new claimant of the throne. This allegiance he never did give in. He was always the faithful servant of those who appointed him, and, whoever might happen to be the temporary master of Britain, regularly addressed his despatches and reports to the central authority in Italy. On the other hand, he did not feel himself bound to take direct steps towards asserting that authority in the island. He had to keep the pirates in check, and that was occupation quite sufficient to keep all his energies employed. Thus, as has been said, he observed a kind of neutrality, always loyal to the Roman Emperor, but willing to be on friendly terms with the rebel generals of Britain as long as they left him alone, let him do his work of defending the coast, and did not make any demands upon him which his conscience would not allow him to satisfy.

Having thus sketched the career of the Count, we must now say something about the house, which now—it was early in the afternoon of the day following the events described in the last chapter—was just coming into sight.

The villa was the Count's private property, and had been purchased by him immediately on his arrival in the island, for a reason which will be given hereafter. It was a handsome house, and complete in its way, with all that was necessary for a comfortable residence, but not one of the largest of its kind. Indeed, it may be said that what may be called the " living " part of it was unusually small for the dwelling of so distinguished a person as the Count. It had been found large enough by its previous owners, men of moderate means and, it so happened, of small families; and the Count, feeling that his occupation of it might be terminated at any time, had not cared to add to it. Its situation was remarkably pleasing.   Behind it was a sheltering range of hills,[1] keeping off the force of the south-westerly winds, and then richly covered with wood.   It was not too near the sea, the Romans not finding that the ceaseless disturbance of rising and falling tides was an element of pleasure, though they could not get too close to their own tideless Mediterranean; but it was within an easy distance of the Haven.[2] The convenience of this neighbourhood had indeed been one of the Count's reasons for selecting this spot.   But if the harsh, grating sound of the waves upon the shingle did not reach the ears of the dwellers in the villa, and the force of the sea winds was somewhat broken for them by intervening cliffs, they still enjoyed all the freshness and vitality of an air that had come across many a league of water. The climate, too, was genial, mild without being too soft, mostly free from damp, though not exempt from occasional mist, seldom troubled by frost or snow, and, on the whole, not unlike some of the more temperate regions of Italy.

The villa, with its belongings, occupied three sides of a square, or rather rectangle, and was built nearly to the points of the compass.   The eastern side of the square was open, thus giving a prospect sea-

---

[1] The hills that run as far as Arreton and the valley of the Medina.

[2] Brading Haven.

wards. The western contained the principal living rooms. The northern, too, was partly occupied by bed-chambers and sitting-rooms, for which there was no room in the comparatively small portion which had been originally intended for the residence of the owner and his family. Some of the workmen employed lived in cottages outside the villa enclosure. The southern was devoted to storehouses, workshops, and all the miscellaneous buildings which made a Roman villa, as far as possible, an establishment complete in itself. The open space was occupied by a pretty garden, which will be more particularly described hereafter.[1]

The eastward front of the villa was occupied for the greater part of its length by a colonnade or corridor. A low wall of about four feet in height separated this from the garden; above the wall it was open to the air ; but an overhanging roof helped greatly to shelter it, while the view into the garden was unimpeded. The floor was adorned with a handsome tesselated pavement, the principal device

---

[1] The villa consisted, it will be seen, of the three parts which were commonly found in establishments of this kind. These were called respectively the *Urbana*, containing the rooms in which the family resided, and including also the garden terraces, &c. ; the *Rustica*, occupied by slaves and workmen but in this case, as will be seen, partly used for another purpose ; and the *Fructuaria*, containing cellars for wine, &c., barns, granaries, and storehouses of various kinds.

of which was a representation of the favourite subject of Orpheus attracting beasts and birds by his
lyre. The proprietor from whom the Count had
purchased the villa had brought it from Italy. He
was a Christian of artistic tastes, and, like his fellow-
believers, had delighted to trace in the old myth a
spiritual meaning, the power of the teaching of
Christ to subdue to the Divine obedience the savage,
animal nature of man. He had displaced for it the
original design, which, indeed, was nothing better
than a commonplace representation of dancing
figures which had satisfied the earlier owners. The
artist had included among the listeners animals.
some of which, as the monkey, the Thracian minstrel
could hardly have seen, and, with a certain touch of
humour, he had adorned the monkey's head with a
Phrygian cap, like that which Orpheus himself
wore, to indicate probably that the monkey is the
caricature of man. The inner wall was ornamented
with a bold design of Cæsar's first landing in
Britain, worked in fresco. Seats and tables were
arranged along it at intervals, and the whole corridor
was thus made to furnish a pleasant promenade in
winter and a charming resort when the weather was
warm.

At the south end of the corridor was the Count's
own apartment, or study, as it would be called in a
modern house. One window looked into the corridor,

into which a door also opened; another, which was built out into the shape of a bow, so as to catch as much of the sun as the aspect allowed, looked into the garden. Part of it was formed of lattices, which admitted of being completely closed when the weather required such protection; the rest was glazed with glass, which would have seemed rough to the present generation, but was quite as good as most people were content to have in their houses fifty years ago. The pavement was tesselated, and presented various designs, a Bacchante, and a pair of gladiators among them. These, however, were commonly covered with thick woollen rugs, the villa being chiefly used as a winter residence. The Count had not forgotten his early studies, and some handsome bookcases contained his favourite authors, among which were to be found the great classic poets of Rome, Tacitus, for whom he had a special regard, some writers on the military art, Cato and Columella on agriculture, and, not least honoured, though some, at least, of their contents had but little interest for him—for, sincere Christian as he was, he cared little for controversy—the numerous treatises of his friend and teacher, Augustine. Behind this room was a simple furnished bed-chamber, showing in an almost bare simplicity the characteristic tastes of a soldier.

At the other end of the corridor was a door leading to the principal chamber in this part of the villa. This measured altogether close upon forty feet in length, but it was divided, or rather could be divided, into two by columns which stood about halfway down its longer sides, and between which a curtain could be hung. When the chamber was occupied in summer it might be used as a whole; in the winter the smaller part, which looked out into the garden, could be shut off from the rest by drawing the curtain, and so made a comfortable room, warmed from below by hot air from the furnace, which had been constructed at the western end of the northern wing of the villa. Much artistic skill had been expended on the pavements of the apartment, and the smaller chamber was very richly decorated in this way. In the middle was a large head of Medusa, and the rest was filled with beautifully-worked scenes illustrating the pleasures of a pastoral life. It was the custom of the Count's family to use the larger portion of the whole chamber as a dining-room, the smaller as a ladies' boudoir. On the rare occasion of some large entertainment being given, the whole was thrown into one.

The ladies of the family, of whom we shall hear more hereafter, had their own apartments at the western end of the north wing, part of which was shut off for their occupation and for their immediate attendants. A covered way connected this with the portion occupied by the Count.

It would be needless to describe the rest of the villa. It was like the houses of its kind, houses which the Romans erected wherever they went in as close an imitation as they could make of what they were accustomed to at home.

The garden, however, must not be wholly passed over. Spacious and handsome as it was, it in part presented a stiff and unnatural appearance, looking, in fact, somewhat theatrical, as contrasted with the pastoral sunniness of the landscape. A Roman gardener had been brought from Rome—one skilled in all the arts of his craft. It was he who had terraced the slope with so much regularity, had planted stiff box hedges—and, above all, it was his taste which led him to cut and train box and laburnum shrubs into fantastic imitations of other forms. The poor trees were forced to abandon their own natural shapes, and to pose as vases, geometrical figures, and animals of various kinds. There was even a ship of box surrounded by a broad channel of water, so that the spectator, making large demands on his imagination, might imagine that the little mock vessel was moored on a still sheet of water. Among the box trees were stone fountains badly copied from classic models. But these had not remained in their bare crudity. The loving British ivy had crept close around them, and added a grace which the sculptor had failed to give. The Roman gardener would have liked to banish this intruder, or to at least train it into the positions prescribed by horticultural rules, but he had been bidden to let it run at its own sweet will; and so it had, and had flourished, well nursed by the soft and humid atmosphere.

Scattered at regular intervals through the green were flower-beds stocked with plants, which were either native to the island, or had been brought hither with great care from the capital. There were roses in several varieties, strange-shaped orchids, which had been found growing wild at lower levels of the island, and adopted into this civilized garden to ornament it with their unique beauty. Gay geraniums and other flowers made throughout the summer bright patches of colour in striking contrast to the dark green.

These beds were enclosed by borders. Between these enclosures were curiously-cut letters of growing box, which perpetuated—at least for the life-time of the shrub—the gardener's own name or that of his master, or classic titles, to serve as designations for certain portions of the place. In the midst of the garden several luxuriant oaks and graceful elms had been allowed to retain in their native freedom the shapes into which they had been growing for so many years. They cast wide shadows, and gave a softened aspect to the unnatural shapes of the trained growths.

Beyond the floral division of the garden was another enclosure for pear and apple trees. They stood on a green sward, soft as velvet, and of a deeper hue than Italian suns permit to the grass on which they smile. Here, too, were foreign embellishments. The monotony of the uniform rows of fruit trees was varied by pyramids of box, and the whole orchard was surrounded by a belt of plane trees.

A circle of oaks had been left at the summit of one of the terraces. Thick hedges were planted between the trees, making a dense wall, in which openings were cut for the view, so that the vista was visible, like a picture set in a dark frame. This green room, roofed by the sky, was paved with a mosaic of the bright coloured chalk from the cliffs at the western end of the island, and contained an oblong basin of water shaped like a table. The water flowed through so gently that the surface always seemed at rest, and yet never grew warm. Couches were placed at this fountain table, and from time to time repasts were served here, certain viands being placed in dishes shaped like swans or boats, which floated gracefully on the watery surface. The more solid meats were placed on the broad marble edges of the basin.

This sylvan retreat seemed made for a meeting of naiads and nereids. In short, the spot was so sheltered, the outlook over sea and land both near and across the strait so fair, that one could well believe even Pliny's famed Tuscan garden, which may have suggested some features of this British one, was not more happily placed.

CHAPTER V.

CARNA.

WHEN Ælius had come, some eighteen years before
the beginning of our story, to take up his command
on the coast of Britain, he had brought with him
his young wife. This lady, always delicate in
health, had not long survived her transplantation to
a northern climate. Six months after her arrival in
Britain she had died in giving birth to a daughter.
The child was entrusted to the care of a British
woman, wife of the sailing master of one of the
Roman ships, who had reared her together with her
own daughter. When little Ælia was but a few
weeks old her foster-mother had become a widow,
her husband having met with his death in a desperate
encounter with one of the Saxon cruisers. This
misfortune had been followed by another, the loss of
her two elder children, who had been carried off by
a malarious fever. The widow, thus doubly bereaved,
had thankfully accepted the Count's offer that she

should take the post of mother of the maids in his household. Her foster-daughter, a feeble little thing, whom she had the greatest difficulty in rearing, was as dear to her as was her own child, and the new arrangement ensured that she should not be separated from her. For ten years she was as happy as a woman who had lost so much could hope to be. She had the pleasure of seeing her delicate nursling pass safely through childhood, and grow into a handsome, vigorous girl. Then her own call came; and feeling that her earthly work was done, she had been glad to meet it. The Count, who was a frequent visitor to her deathbed, had no difficulty in promising her that the two children should never be separated. Indeed he could not have divided the pair even had he wished. Every wish of the ten-year-old Ælia was as a law to him, and Ælia would have simply broken her heart to lose her playmate and sister Carna.

The two friends were curiously unlike in person and disposition. Ælia was a Roman of the Romans. Her hair was of a shining blue-black hue, and so abundant that when unbound it fell almost to her knees. Her black eyes, soft and lustrous in repose, and shaded with lashes of the very longest, could give an almost formidable flash when anything had roused her to anger. Her complexion was a rich brown, relieved by a slight ruddy tinge ; her features regular, less delicately carved, indeed, than the Greek type, but full of expression, which was tender or fiery, according to her mood. Her figure was somewhat small, but beautifully formed. If Ælia was unmistakably Roman, Carna showed equally clearly one of the finest British types. She was tall, overtopping her companion by at least a head; her hair, which fell in curls about her shoulders, was of a glossy chestnut; her eyes of the very deepest blue; her complexion, half-way between blonde and brunette, mantled with a delicate colour, which deepened, when her emotions were touched, into an exquisite blush; her forehead was somewhat low, but broad, and with a rare promise both of artistic power and of intelligence; her nose would have been pronounced by a casual observer to be the most faulty feature in her face; and it is true that its outline was not perfect. But the same observer, after a brief acquaintance, would probably have retracted his censure, and owned that this feature suited the rest of her face, and would have been less charming if it had been more perfect. Ælia was impulsive and quick of temper, honest and affectionate, but not caring to go below the surface of things, and without a particle of imagination. Carna, on the other hand, seemed the gentlest of women. Those blue eyes of hers were ready to express affection and pity; but no one—not even Ælia, who could be exceedingly provoking at times—had ever seen a flash of anger in them.   But her nature had depths in it that none suspected to be there ; it was richly endowed with all the best gifts of her Celtic race. She had a world of her own with which the gay Roman girl, whom she loved so dearly, and with whom she seemed to share all her thoughts, had nothing to do.   Music touched her soul in a way of which Ælia, who could sing very charmingly, and play with no little expression on the *cithara*, had no conception.   And though she had never written, or even composed, a verse, and possibly would never write or compose one, she was a poetess.   At present all her soul was given to religion, religion full of the imagination and enthusiasm which has made saints of so many women of her race.   The good British priest, to whose flock she belonged, a worthy man who eked out his scanty income [1] by working a small farm, was perplexed by her enthusiasm.   She was not satisfied with the duties of adorning the little church where he ministered, and its humble altar-cloths and vestments, by the skill of her nimble fingers, of aiding the chants with the rich tones of her beautiful voice, of ministering to the sick.   She performed these, indeed, with devotion, but she demanded more, and the good man did not know how to satisfy her.

In addition to her other gifts Carna had that of being

---

[1] The British bishops were notoriously poor, and their clergy were doubtless still more slenderly provided for.

a born nurse. It was her first impulse to fly to the help of anything—whether it was man, or beast, or bird—that was sick or hurt, just as it was Ælia's impulse, though she mastered it at any strong call of duty, to avoid the sight of suffering. She had now heard that a prisoner had been brought in desperately wounded, and she could not rest till she knew whether she could do anything for the poor creature's soul or body. Ælia was as scornful as her love for her foster-sister allowed her to be.

" My dearest Carna," she cried, " what on earth can make you trouble yourself in this fashion about this miserable creature? They are the worst plagues in this world, these Saxons, and it would be a blessing to the world if it were well quit of the whole race of them! A set of pagan dogs ! "

" Oh, sister," said Carna, her eyes brimming with tears, " that is the worst of it. A pagan, who has never heard of the Blessed Lord, and now, they say, he is dying ! What shall we do for him ? "

" But surely," returned the other, " he is no worse off than his threescore companions who went to the bottom the other day."

" God be good to them," said Carna, " but then we did not know them, and that seems to make a difference. And to think that this poor creature should be so near to the way and not find it. But I must go and see him."

" It will only tear your poor, tender heart for no purpose. You had far better come and talk to father."

Carna was not to be persuaded, but hurried to the chamber to which the wounded man had been borne.

It was evident at first sight that the end was not far off. The dying Saxon lay stretched on a rude pallet. He was a young man, who could scarcely have seen as many as twenty summers, for the down was hardly to be seen on his upper lip and chin. His face, which was curiously fair for one who had followed from infancy an outdoor life, was deadly pale, a pathetic contrast with the red-gold hair which fell in curly profusion about it. His eyes, in which the fire was almost quenched, were wide open, and fixed with an unchanging gaze upon a figure that stood motionless at the foot of the bed. This was his brother, who had been permitted by the humanity of the Count to be present. They had been exchanging a few sentences, but the dying man was now too far gone to speak, and the two could only look their last farewell to each other. It was a pitiful thing to see the twins, so like in feature and form, but now so different, the one, prisoner as he was, full of life and strength, the other on the very threshold of death.

By the side of the wounded man stood the household physician, a venerable-looking slave, who had acquired such knowledge of medicine and surgery as sufficed for the treatment of the commoner ailments and accidents. This case was beyond his skill, or indeed the skill of any man. He could do nothing but from time to time put a few drops of cordial between the sufferer's lips. Next to the physician stood the priest, and his skill, too, seemed to be at fault. A messenger, sent by Carna, had warned him that a dying man required his ministrations, but had added no further particulars, and the worthy man, who was busy at the time in littering down his cattle, had hastily changed his working dress for his priestly habiliments, and had come ready, as he thought, to administer the last consolations of the Church to a dying Christian. The case utterly perplexed him. He had tried the two languages with which he was familiar, and found them useless. No one had been able to understand a single word of the dialogue which had passed between the brothers. The dying stranger was as hopelessly separated from him and the means of grace that he could command as if he had been a thousand miles away. He could not even venture—for his theology was of the narrowest type—to commend to the mercy of God the passing soul of this unbaptized heathen.

Carna understood the situation at a glance. She saw death in the Saxon's face ; she saw the hopeless perplexity in the expression of the priest.

" Father," she cried, " can you do nothing, nothing at all for this poor soul ? "

" My daughter," said the priest, " I am helpless. He knows nothing ; he understands nothing."

" Can you not baptize him ? "

" Baptize him without a profession of repentance, without a confession of faith !   Impossible ! "

" Will you let him perish before your eyes without an effort to save him ? "

" Child," said the priest, with some impatience in his tone, " I have told you that I am helpless.   It was not I that brought these things about."

The girl cast an agonized look about the room, as of one that appealed for help, and seized a crucifix that hung upon the wall.   She threw herself upon her knees by the bedside, and after pressing the symbol of Redemption passionately to her lips, held it to the mouth of the dying man.   The Saxon, on his first entrance into the room, had removed his look from his brother and fixed it steadfastly on this beautiful apparition.   Clad in white from head to foot, with a golden girdle about her waist, her eyes shining with excitement, her whole face transfigured by a passion of pity, she seemed to him a vision from another world, one of the Walhalla maidens of whom his mother had talked to him in days gone by. His lips closed feebly on the crucifix which she held to them ; a smile lighted up his fading eyes, and he muttered with his last breath "Valkyria." The girl heard the word and remembered without understanding it. The next moment he was dead, and one of the women standing by stepped forward and closed his eyes.

Carna burst into a passion of tears.

"He is gone," she cried, amidst her sobs, "he is gone, and we could not help him."

The priest was silent. He had no consolation to offer. Indeed, but that he recognized the girl's saintliness—a saintliness to which he, worthy man as he was, had no pretensions—he would have thought her grief foolish. But the old physician could not keep silence.

"Pardon me, lady," he said, "if I seem to reprove you. I pray you not to suffer your zeal for the salvation of souls to overpower your faith. Do you think that the All-Father does not love this poor stranger as well as you, nay, better than you can love him? that He cannot care for him as well? that you, forsooth, must save him out of His hands? Nay, my daughter—pardon an old man for the word—do not so distrust Him."

"You are right, father, as always," said the girl. "I have been selfish and faithless. I was angry, I suppose, to find myself baffled and helpless. You must set me a penance, father," she added, turning to the priest.

The Saxon meanwhile had contrived by his gestures to make his guards understand that he wished to take his farewell of his dead brother. They allowed him to approach the bed. He stooped and kissed the lips of the dead, and then, choking down the sobs which convulsed his breast, turned away, seemingly calm and unmoved. But as he passed Carna he contrived to catch with his manacled hands one of the flowing sleeves of her white robe, and to lift the hem to his lips.

CHAPTER VI.

IT was not easy to know what should be done with the survivor of the two Saxon captives. The villa had no proper provision for the safe custody of prisoners; and the problem of keeping a man under lock and key, without a quite disproportionate amount of trouble, was as difficult as it would be in the ordinary country house of modern times.

"I shall send him to the camp at the Great Harbour," said the Count, a few days after the scene described in our last chapter. "It is quite impossible to keep him unless we chain him hand and foot, or set half a dozen men to guard him; and even then he is such a giant that he might easily overpower them. At the camp they have got a prison, and stocks which would hold him as fast as death."

Carna's face clouded over when she heard the Count's determination, but she said nothing. The lively Ælia broke in—

"My dear father, you will break poor Carna's heart if you do anything of the kind. She is bent on making a convert of the noble savage. And anyhow, whatever else she may induce him to worship, he seems ready, from what I have seen, to worship her. And besides, what harm can he do? He has no arms, and he can't speak a word of any language known here. If he were to run away he would either be killed or be starved to death."

"Well, Carna," said the Count, with a smile, "what do you say? Will you stand surety for this young pagan? Or shall I make him your slave, and then, if he runs away, it will be your loss?"

"I hope," said the girl, "that you won't send him to the camp, where, I fear, they hold the lives of such as he very cheap."

"Well," replied the Count, "we will keep him here, at all events for the present, and I will give the bailiff orders to give him something to do in the safest place that he can think of."

Accordingly the young Saxon was set to work at the forge attached to the villa, and proved himself a willing and serviceable labourer. No more suitable choice, indeed, could have been made. That he was a man of some rank at home everything about him seemed to show—nothing more than his hands, which were delicate, and unusually small in proportion to his almost gigantic stature. But the

CEDRIC AT THE FORGE.

greatest chief among his people would not have disdained the hammer and anvil. Was not Thor a mighty smith? And was it not almost as much a great warrior's business to make a good sword as to wield it well when it was made? So the young man, whose mighty shoulders and muscular arms were regarded with respect and even astonishment by his British fellow-workmen, laboured with a will, showing himself no mean craftsman in the blacksmith's art. Sometimes, as he plied the hammer, he would chant to himself, in a low voice, what sounded like a war-song. Otherwise he remained absolutely silent, not even attempting to pick up the few common words which daily intercourse with his companions gave him the opportunity of learning. There was an air of dignity about him which seemed to forbid any of the little affronts to which a prisoner would naturally be exposed; his evidently enormous strength, too, was a thing which even the most stupid of his companions respected. Silent, self-contained, and impassive, he moved quietly about his daily tasks; it was only when he caught a glimpse of Carna that his features were lighted up for a moment with a smile.

The idea of opening up any communication with him seemed hopeless, when an unexpected, but still quite natural, way out of the difficulty presented itself. An old peddler, who was accustomed to supply the inmates of the villa with silks and jewellery, and who sometimes had a book in his pack for Carna, paid in due course one of his periodical visits. The old man was a Gaul by birth, a native of one of the States on the eastern bank of the Rhine, and in youth he had been an adventurous trader, extending his journeys eastward and northward as far as the shores of the Baltic. The risk was great, for the Germans of the interior looked with suspicion on the visits of civilized strangers; but, on the other hand, the profits were considerable. Amber, in pieces of a size and clearness seldom matched on the coasts of Gaul and Britain, and beautiful furs, as of the seal and the sea-otter, could be bought at very low prices from these unsophisticated tribes, and sold again to the wealthy ladies of Lutetia [1] and Lugdunum [2] at a very considerable advantage. In these wanderings Antrix—for that was the peddler's name—had acquired a good knowledge of the language—substantially the same, though divided into several dialects—spoken by the German tribes; and, indeed, without such knowledge his trading adventures would have been neither safe nor profitable. As he approached old age Antrix had judged it expedient to transfer his business from Gaul to Britain. Gaul

---

[1] Lutetia Parisiorum, now Paris.   [2] Now Lyons.

he found to be a dangerous place for a peaceable trader, having lost more than once all the profits of a journey, and, indeed, a good deal more, by one of the marauding bands by whom the country was periodically overrun. Britain, or at least the southern district of Britain, was certainly safer, and it was this that for the last ten years he had been accustomed to traverse, till he had become a well-known and welcome visitor at every villa and settlement along the coast.

Here then chance, or, as Carna preferred to think, Providence, had provided an interpreter; and it so happened that, whether by another piece of good fortune, or an additional interposition, his services were made permanently useful. The old man had found his journeys becoming in the winter too laborious for his strength, and it was not very difficult to persuade him to make his home in the villa for two or three months till the severity of the season should have passed. Every one was pleased at the arrangement. Antrix was an admirable teller of tales, and his had been an adventurous life, full of incident, with which he knew how to make the winter night less long. The Count saw a rare opportunity, such as had never come to him before, of learning something about the hardy freebooters whom it was his business to overawe; and Carna had the liveliest hopes of making a proselyte, if she could only make herself, and the message in which she had so profound a faith, understood.

The young Saxon's resolution and pride did not long hold out against the unexpected delight of being able once more to converse in his own language, and he soon began to talk with perfect freedom — for, he had no idea of having anything to conceal— about his home and his people. He was the son, they learnt from him, of the chief of one of the Saxon settlements near the mouth of the Albis.[1] The people lived by hunting and fishing, and, more or less, by cultivating the soil. But life was hard. The settlements were crowded; game was growing scarce, and had to be followed further afield every year; the climate, too, was very uncertain, and the crops sometimes failed altogether. In short, they could not live without what they were able to pick up in their expeditions to richer countries and more temperate climates. On this point the young Saxon was perfectly frank. The idea that there was anything of which a warrior could possibly be ashamed in taking what he could by the strong hand had evidently never crossed his mind. To rob a neighbour or fellow-tribesman he counted shameful—so much could be gathered from expressions that he let drop; as to others, his simple morality was this—to keep what you had, to take what others could not keep.

[1] The Elbe.

The Count found him curiously well informed on what may be called the politics of Europe. He was well aware of the decay of the Roman power. Kinsmen and neighbours of his own had made their way south to get their share in the spoil of the Empire. Some, he had heard, had stopped to take service with the enemy; some had come back with marvellous tales of the wealth and luxury which they had seen. About Britain itself he had very clear views. The substance of what he said to the Count was this: "You won't stop here very long. My father says that you have been weakening your fleet and armies here for years past, and that you will soon take them away altogether. Then we shall come and take the country. It will hardly be in his time, he says. Perhaps it may not be in mine. It is only you that hinder us; it is only you that we are afraid of. We shall have the island; we must have it. Our own country is too small and too barren to keep us."

Of his own adventures the young Saxon had little to say. This was the first voyage that he and his brother had taken. Their father was in failing health, and their mother, who had but one other child, a girl some ten years younger, had kept them at home, till she had been unwillingly persuaded that they were losing caste by taking no part in the warlike excursions of their countrymen. " We had a fairly successful time," went on the young chief, with the absolute un-consciousness of wrong with which a hunter might relate his exploits; "took two merchantmen that had good cargoes on board, and had a right royal fight with the people of a town on the Gallic coast. We killed thirty of them; and only five of our warriors went to the Walhalla. Then we turned homeward, but our ship struck on a rock near some islands far to the west,[1] and had almost gone to the bottom. With great labour we dragged her ashore, and set to work repairing her; but our chief smith and carpenter had fallen in the battle, and we were a long time in making her fit for sea. This was the reason why we were going home so late, and also why we lagged behind our comrades when you were chasing us. By rights we were the best crew and had the swiftest ship, but she had been clumsily mended, and dragged terribly in the water."

The Count listened to all this with the greatest interest, and plied the speaker with questions, all of which he answered with perfect frankness. He found out how many warriors the settlement could muster, what were the relations with their neighbours, whether there had been any definite plans for a common expedition. On the whole, he came to the conclusion that though there was no danger of an overpowering

---

[1] Probably the Channel Islands, always a dangerous place for navigation.

migration from this quarter such as Western and Southern Europe had suffered from in former times, these sea-faring tribes of the East would be an increasing danger to Britain as years went on. Personally the prospect did not concern him greatly; his fortunes were not bound up with the island. Still he loved the place and its people; it troubled him to see what dark days were in store for them. And taking a wider view—for he was a man of large sympathies—he was grieved to see another black cloud in an horizon already so dark. Would anything civilized be left, he thought to himself, when every part of Europe has been swept by these hosts of barbarians?

Before long another source of interest was discovered in the young Saxon. The Count happened to overhear him chanting to himself, and though he could not distinguish the words, he recognized in the rhythm something like the camp-songs that he had often listened to from German warriors in Stilicho's camp. Here again the peddler's services as an interpreter were put in requisition, and though the old man's Latin, which went little beyond his practical wants as a trader, fell lamentably short of what was wanted, enough was heard to interest the villa family, which had a literary turn, very much. What the young man had sung to himself was an early Saga, a curious romance [1] of heroes fighting with monsters,

---

[1] Perhaps something like the early Saxon poem which we know under the name of Beowulf.

as unlike as can be conceived to anything to be found in Roman poetry—verse in its rudest shape, but still making itself felt as a real poet's work.

Lastly, Carna, now that she had found a way of communicating her thoughts, threw herself with ardour into the work of proselytizing the stranger. Here the peddler was more at home in his task as interpreter. Carna used the dialect of South Britain, with which he was far more familiar than he was with Latin—it differed indeed but little from his native speech. The topics too were familiar, for he had been brought up in the Christian faith, and though he scarcely understood the girl's zeal, he was quite willing to help her as much as he could.

Carna found her task much more difficult than she had expected. She had thought in her simple faith that it would be enough for her to tell to the young heathen the story of the Crucified Christ for him to fall down at once and worship. He listened with profound attention and respect. This, perhaps, he would have accorded to anything that came from her lips ; but, beyond this, the story itself profoundly interested him. But it must be confessed that there was a good deal in it which did not commend itself to his warrior's ideal of what the God whom he could worship should be. He was a soldier, and he could scarcely conceive of anything great or good that was outside a soldier's virtues. The gods of his own

heaven, Odin and Thor and Balder, were great conquerors, armed with armour which no mortal blow
could pierce, wielders of sword and hammer which
were too heavy for any mortal arm to wield. He
could bow down to them because they were greater,
immeasurably greater than himself, in the qualities
and gifts which he most honoured. Now he was
called upon to receive a quite different set of ideas, to
set up a quite different standard of excellence. The
story of the Gospels touched him. It roused him
almost to fury when he heard how the good man who
had gone about healing the sick and feeding the hungry had been put shamefully to death by His own
countrymen, by those who knew best what He had
done. If Carna had bidden him avenge the man
who had been so ungratefully treated, he would have
performed her bidding with pleasure. But to worship
this Crucified One, to depose for Him Odin, Lord of
Battles—that seemed impossible.

Still he was impressed, and impressed chiefly by
the way in which the preacher seemed to translate
into her own life the principles of the faith which she
tried to set forth to him. She had told him that this
Crucified One had died for him. He could not understand why He should have done so, why He should
not have led His twelve legions of angels against the
wicked, swept them off from the face of the earth,
and established by force of arms a kingdom of justice.

Still the idea of so much having been given, so much endured for his sake touched him, especially when he saw how passionately in earnest was this wonderful creature, this beautiful prophetess, as, with the German reverence for women, he was ready to regard her, how eager she was to do him good, how little, as he could not but feel, she thought of herself in comparison with others.

As long as Carna dwelt on these topics she made good way; when she wandered away from them, as naturally she sometimes did, she was not so successful. One day it unluckily occurred to her that she would appeal to his fears.

" Do not refuse to listen," she said to him, "for if He is infinitely good to those who love Him, He can also be angry with those who love Him not."

" What will He do with them ?" asked the young Saxon.

" He will send them to suffer in everlasting fire."

" Ah !" answered the youth, " I have heard from our wise men of such a place into which Odin drives cowards, and oath-breakers, and such as are false to their friends. But they say it is a place of everlasting cold, and this indeed seems to me to be worse than fire."

" Yes," said Carna, " there is such a place of torment, and it is kept not only for the wicked, as you say, but for all who do not believe."

" Will the Lord Christ then banish thither all who do not own Him as their Master, and call themselves by His name ? "

" Yes—and think how terrible a thing it would be if it should happen to you."

" And that is why you are so anxious to persuade me ? "

" Yes."

" And why you were so troubled about my brother when you could not make him understand before he died ? "

" Yes. Oh ! it was dreadful to think he should pass away when safety was in his reach."

" And you think that the Lord Christ has sent him to that place because he did not know Him ? "

" I fear that it must be so."

" Then He shall send me also. For how am I better because I have lived longer ? No—I will be with my brother, whom I loved, and with my own people."

And neither for that day nor for many days to come would he speak again on this subject. Carna was greatly troubled ; but she began to think whether there might not be something in what the young man had said.

CHAPTER VII.

A PRETENDER'S DIFFICULTIES.

OUR story must now go back a little, and take up the course of events at the camp, where the look of affairs was not promising. The donative promised by Constantine on the day of his election had been paid, but this had been done only after the greatest exertions in wringing money out of unlucky traders, farmers, and even peasants, who had been already squeezed almost dry. All that had any coin left were beginning to bury it,[1] and though the collectors of taxes, or loans, or gifts, or whatever else the frequent requisition of money might be called, had ingenious ways of discovering or making their owners give up these hoards, it was quite evident that very little more could be got out of Britain. The military chest meanwhile was becoming alarmingly empty,

---

[1] Possibly the reason why so much buried money belonging to the later days of the Roman occupation of Britain has been found.

and though money was still found somehow for the larger camps, some of the less important garrisons had been left for months with almost nothing in the way of pay. What was to be done was a pressing question, which had to be answered in some way within a few days. If it was not so answered, it was tolerably plain that Constantine would meet the fate of Marcus and Gratianus. The Emperor himself (if we are to give him this title) seemed to be very little troubled by the prospect, and remained stolidly calm. His elevation indeed had made the least possible difference to him. He drank a better kind of wine, and perhaps a little more—for his cups had been limited by his means—but he did not run into excess. He was still the same simple, contented, good-natured man that he had always been. But his sons were of another temper, though curiously differing from each other. Constans the elder was an enthusiast, almost a fanatic, a man of strong religious feeling, who would have followed the religious life if it had been possible, and who now, finding himself possessed of power, had schemes of using it to promote his favourite schemes. Julian the younger had ambitions of a more commonplace kind. But both the brothers were agreed in holding on to the power that had been so strangely put into their father's hands, hands which, as he had very little will of his own, were practically theirs.

A council was held at which Constantine, his two sons, and three of the officers of highest rank were present, and the urgent question of the day was anxiously debated.

Julian began the discussion.

"The army," he said, "must be employed, or it will find mischief to do at home which all of us will be sorry for."

"I have some one to introduce to your Majesty," said one of the officers present, "who may have something to say which will influence your decision. He is from Ierne,[1] and brings me a letter from the commander at Uriconium. He came last night."

"Let him enter," said Constantine, with his usual dull phlegmatic voice.

The tribune went to the door of the chamber, and despatched a message to his quarters. In a few minutes the stranger was introduced into the council. He was a man verging upon middle age, somewhat short of stature, with a great bush of fiery-red hair, which stood up from his head with a very fierce look, a long, shaggy beard of the same colour, eyes of the deepest blue, very bright and piercing, but with a

---

[1] Ireland. A similar incident is mentioned by Tacitus in his life of Agricola. An Irish petty king, driven from his throne by internal troubles, came to the Roman general and promised, if he were restored, to bring the island under the dominion of Rome. This is the first notice of the country that occurs in history.

wandering and unsteady look in them, and a ruddy complexion which deepened to an intense colour on his cheek bones and other prominent parts of his face. Around his neck he wore a heavy twisted collar of remarkably red gold. Massive rings of the same metal adorned his fingers. His dress was of un-dyed wool, and very rudely shaped, a curious contrast to the richness of his ornaments. He was followed into the room by an interpreter, a young native of Northern Britain, who had been carried off by Irish pirates from one of the ecclesiastical schools. He had been taught Latin before his captivity, and, while a captive, had made himself acquainted with the Irish language, which indeed did not differ very much from that spoken in Britain.[1] His task of interpreter was not by any means an easy one to fulfil. The Prince broke out into a rapid torrent of complaint, invective, and entreaty, which left the young man, who was not very expert in either of the languages with which he had to deal, hopelessly behind. Then seeing that he was not followed, he turned on his unlucky attendant and dealt him a blow upon the ear that sent him staggering across the room. Then he seemed to remember himself, and began to tell his story again at a more moderate rate of speed, though he still from time to time, when he came to

---

[1] This was exactly what had happened not many years before to St. Patrick, the Apostle of Ireland.

some peculiarly exciting part in the tale of his wrongs, broke out into a rapid eloquence that baffled all interpretation. The upshot of the story was this—

He was, or rather had been, a small king in South-eastern Ireland,[1] the eldest of four brothers, having succeeded his father about ten years before. There had been a quarrel about the division of some property. The Prince was a little obscure in his description of the property; indeed it was a matter about which he was shrewd enough to say as little as possible. But his hearers had no difficulty in presuming that it consisted of spoil carried off from Britain. The quarrel had come to blows. All the nation had been divided into parties in the dispute. Finally he had been compelled by his ungrateful subjects to fly for his life. Would the Emperor bring him back? He was liberal, even extravagant, in his offers. He would bring the whole island under his dominion. (As a matter of fact, his dominions had never reached more than seventy miles inland, and he had contrived to make himself so hated during his ten years' reign that he had scarcely a friend or follower left.) And what an island it was! There never was such a place. The sheep were fatter, the cows gave more milk than in any other place in the whole world. And there was

---

[1] Probably somewhere near Wexford.

gold too, gold to be had for the picking up; and amber on the shores, and pearls in the rivers. In short, it was a treasure-house of wealth, which was waiting for the lucky first-comer.

" Are you a Christian ? " asked Constans.

The exiled chief would have gladly said that he was, and indeed for a moment thought of the audacious fiction that his attachment to the new faith had been one of the causes of his expulsion. He was, in fact, a savagely bigoted pagan, and had dealt very roughly with one or two missionaries who had ventured into his neighbourhood. But he reflected that the falsehood would infallibly be detected, and would inevitably do him a great deal of harm.

" No ! " he exclaimed; " would that I were. But there is nothing that I so much desire if only I could attain to that blessing. But I promise to be baptized myself, and to have every man, woman, and child within my dominions baptized within a month, if you will only bring me back to them."

Even Constans thought this zeal to be a little excessive.

" And how many men can you bring into the field ? " asked the more practical Julian ; " and what money can you find for the pay of the soldiers ? "

The stranger was taken aback at these direct questions.

"All my subjects, all my treasures are yours," he said, after a pause.

"I don't believe," said one of the tribunes in Latin to Julian, "that he has any subjects besides this wretched interpreter, or any treasure beyond what he wears on his neck and his fingers."

"Shall he withdraw?" said Julian to his father.

Constantine, who never spoke when he could avoid speaking, answered by a nod, and the Irish Prince withdrew.

"Let us have nothing to do," said the practical Julian, "with these Irish savages. They may cut their own throats, and welcome, without our helping them. The men, too, would rebel at the bare mention of Ierne. It is out of the world in their eyes, and I think they are about right. And as to the gold and pearls, I don't believe in them."

"Perhaps you are right," asid Constans; "but it would be a great work to bring over a new nation to the orthodox faith."

Julian answered with a laugh. "My good brother, we are not all such zealous missionaries as you. I am afraid that preaching is not exactly the work which our friends the soldiers are looking out for."

"What does your Majesty say to an expedition to chastise those thieving Picts? They grow more insolent every day."

This was the suggestion of one of the tribunes.

"What is to be got?" was Julian's answer.

"Glory!" answered the tribune.

"Glory! What is that?—the men want pay and plunder. These bare-legged villains haven't so much as a rag that you can take from them, and they have a shrewd way of giving at least as many hard blows as they take. No!—we will leave the Picts alone, and only too thankful if they will do the same for us!"

"The Count of the Shore has not yet taken the oath to his Majesty," said an officer who had not spoken before. "We might give some employment to the men in bringing him to reason."

Constantine spoke for the first time since the council had begun its sitting—"The Count is a good man and does his business well. Leave him alone."

Other suggestions were made and discussed without any sensible approach to a conclusion, and the council broke up, but with an understanding that it should meet again with as little delay as possible.

On the afternoon of that very day an incident occurred which convinced every one—if further conviction was needed—that delay would certainly be fatal.

A party of soldiers was practising javelin throwing, and Constantine, who had been particularly expert in this exercise in his youth, stood watching the game. He had stepped up to examine the mark made by one of the weapons on the wooden figure at which the men were throwing, when a javelin passed most perilously near his head and buried itself in the wood. It could not have been an accident; no one could have been so recklessly careless as to throw under the circumstances. Constantine was as imperturbable as usual. Without a sign of fear or anger, he said, "Comrades, you mistake; I am not made of wood," and, signing to his attendants, walked quietly away. The incident, however, made a great impression upon him, and a still greater upon his sons.

The consultation was renewed and prolonged far into the night, and, as no conclusion was reached, continued on the next day. About noon an unexpected adviser appeared upon the scene.

A message was brought into the council-chamber that a merchant from Gaul had something of importance to communicate to the Emperor. The man was admitted, after having been first searched by way of precaution. His dress was sober in cut and colour, and he had a small pack such as the wandering dealers in jewellery and similar light articles were accustomed to carry. Otherwise he was little like a trader; indeed, it did not need a very acute or practised hand to detect in him a soldier's bearing, and even that of one who was accustomed to command.

JAVELIN THROWING.

" You have something to tell us ? " said Julian.

" Yes, I have," said the stranger, " but let me first show you my credentials."

He spoke in passable Latin, but with a decided accent, which, strongly marked as it was, was not recognized by any of those present. At the same time he produced from a silken purse, which he wore like a girdle round his waist, a small square of parchment. It was a letter written in a minute but very clear hand, and it had evidently been put for the security of the bearer, who could thus more easily dispose of it in case of need, into the smallest possible compass. This was handed to Constantine, who, in turn, passed it on to his elder son Constans, he being the only one present who could read and write with fluency. It ran thus:

" Alaric, the son of Baltha, King of the Goths, Emperor of the World, to Marcus, Emperor of Britain and the West, greeting."

A grim smile passed over Constantine's face as he heard this address. He muttered to himself, " ' Marcus,' indeed ! Those who write to the Emperor of Britain must have speedy letter-carriers. The letter proceeded thus:

" I desire friendship and alliance with the nations who are wearied and worn out with the oppressions and cruelties of Rome, and for this purpose send this present by my

*trusty kinsman and counsellor Atualphus, to you who are,
I understand, asserting against the common tyrant of the
world the liberty of Britain and the West.   I have not
thought it fit to trust more to writing, but commend to
you the bearer hereof, the aforesaid Atualphus, who is
acquainted with the mind and purpose of myself and of
my people, and with whom you may conveniently concert
such plans as may best serve our common welfare.   Farewell.   Given at my camp at Æmona."*

"Marcus is no more," said Julian.   "He was
unworthy of his dignity.   You are in the presence of
the most excellent Constantine, Emperor of Britain."

"It matters not," said the Goth, with a haughty
smile.   "My lord the king will treat as willingly
with one as with another, so he be an enemy of
Rome!"

"And what does he propose?   What would he
have us do?"

"Make common cause with him against Honorius
and Rome."

"What shall we gain thereby?"

"Half of the Empire of the World."

"How shall that be?"

"The King will march into Italy and attack the
Emperor in his own land.   The Emperor will withdraw all the legions that he yet controls for his own
defence.   With them the King will deal.   Then

comes your opportunity. What does it profit you to remain in this island, where nothing is to be won either of glory or of riches. Cross over into Gaul and Spain, which, wearied with oppression and desiring above all things to throw off the Roman yoke, will gladly welcome you. Your Cæsar shall reign on this side of the Alps and the Pyrenees. The future may bring other things, but that may suffice for the present."

The plan, so bold, and yet, it would seem, so feasible, and presenting a ready escape out of a situation that seemed hopeless, struck every one present with a delighted surprise. Even the phlegmatic Constantine was roused. " It shall be done," he said.

Some further conversation followed, which it is not necessary to relate. Ways and means were discussed. Questions were asked about the strength and temper of the forces in Gaul and Spain, about the feeling of the towns, and a hundred other matters, with all of which Atualphus showed a curiously intimate knowledge. When the Goth retired from the council, he left very little doubt or hesitation behind him.

"They are heretics—these Goths," grumbled Constans; "obstinate Arians every one of them, I told——"

" You shall convert them, my brother," answered

Julian, "when you are Bishop of Rome. When we divide the West between us, that shall be your portion."

"It shall be done," said Constantine again, as he rose from his chair.

CHAPTER VIII.

THE NEWS IN THE CAMP.

THAT afternoon a banquet, which was as handsomely set out as the very short notice permitted, was given to all the officers in the camp. When the tables were removed,[1] Constantine, who had been carefully primed by his sons with what he was to say, addressed his guests. His words were few and to the point. "Britain," he said, "has been long enough ruled by others. It is now time that she should begin herself to rule. It was the error of those who went before me to be content with the limits of this island. But here there is not enough to content us. Beyond the sea, separated from us by only a few hours' journey, lie wealthy provinces which wait for our coming. A kindlier sky, more fertile fields, richer and fairer cities than ours are there. We have only to show ourselves, in short, to be both

---

[1] With us tables are cleared after a meal ; with the Romans they seem to have been actually removed.

welcomed and obeyed.   Half the victories which we have won here to no profit over poverty-stricken barbarians would have sufficed to give us riches even beyond our desires.   Henceforth let us use our arms where they may win something for us beyond empty honour and wounds.   Follow me, and within a year you shall be masters both of Gaul and Spain."

The younger guests received this oration with shouts of applause ; visions of promotion and prize-money, and even of the spoil of some of the wealthy cities of the mainland floated before them.   The older men did not show this enthusiasm.   Many of them were attached to Britain by ties that they were very loth to break.   They had little to hope, but much to fear, from a change.   Still, they saw the necessity for doing something ; another year such as that which had just passed would thoroughly demoralize the army of Britain.   Legions that get into the habit of making emperors and killing them for their pastime must be dealt with by vigorous remedies, and the easiest and best of these was active service.   In any case it would have been impolitic to show dissent. Many feigned, therefore, a joy which they did not feel, and shouted approval when the Senior Tribune exclaimed, " Comrades, drink to our chief, Constantine Augustus, Emperor of Britain and the West."

The revel was kept up late into the night, the young Goth distinguishing himself by the marvellous depth of his draughts and the equally marvellous strength of his head.

The Emperor retired early from the scene, and Constans, who had little liking for these boisterous scenes, followed his example, as did most of the older men. One of these, the cheery centurion, who has been mentioned more than once, we may follow to his home.

Outside the camp had grown up a village of considerable size, though it consisted for the most part of humble dwellings. There were two or three taverns, or rather drinking-shops, where the soldiers could carouse on the thin, sour wine of the British vineyards, or, if the length of their purses permitted, on metheglin, a more potent drink, made from the fermentation of honey. A Jew, driven by the restless speculation of his race, had established himself in a shop where he sold cheap ornaments to the soldiers' wives, and advanced money to their husbands on the security of their pay. A tailor displayed tunics and cloaks, and a shoemaker sold boots warranted to resist the cold and wet of the island climate. There were a few cottages occupied by the grooms and stablemen who attended to the horses employed in the camp, by fishermen who plied their trade in the neighbouring waters, and other persons of a variety of miscellaneous employments in one way or other connected with the camp. But just outside the main street, at the end nearest to the camp, stood a house of somewhat greater pretensions. It was indeed a humble imitation of the Roman villa, being built round three sides of an irregular square, which was itself occupied by a grass plot and a few flower beds. It was to this that the Centurion Decius bent his steps after the conversation related in the last chapter. It was evidently with the reluctant step of the bearer of bad news that he proceeded on his way. As soon as he entered the enclosure his approach was observed from within. Two blooming girls, whose ages may have been seventeen and fifteen respectively, ran gaily to meet him. A woman some twenty-five years older, but still youthful of aspect and handsome, followed at a more sober pace.

" What is the matter, father? " cried the elder of the girls, who had been quick to perceive that all was not right.

The centurion held up his hand and made a signal for silence. "Hush," he said ; " I have something to tell you, but it must not be here. Let us go indoors."

" Shall the children leave us alone ? " said the centurion's wife, who had now come up.

" No," he answered, wearily, " let them be with us while they can," he added in a low voice, which only the wife's ears, made keenly alive by affection and fear, could catch.

The gaiety of the young people was quenched,

for, without having any idea of what had happened, they could see plainly enough that something was disturbing their parents ; and it was with fast beating hearts that they waited for his explanation.

" Our happy days here are over, my dearest," said the centurion, drawing his wife to him, and tenderly kissing her, as soon as they were within doors.

" You mean," said she, " that the order has come."

" Yes," he answered, " we are to leave as soon as the transports can be collected. The resolution was made to-day and will be announced to the army to-morrow. It is no secret, I suppose, or will not be for long.'

" And where are we to go ? " cried the elder of the girls, whose face brightened as the thought of seeing a little more of the world, of a home in one of the cities of Gaul, possibly in Rome itself, flitted across her mind.

The poor centurion changed colour. The girl's question brought up the difficulty which he knew had to be faced, but which he would gladly have put off as long as he could.

" We shall go to Gaul, certainly ; where I cannot say," he answered, after a long pause, and in a hesitating voice.

" Oh, how delightful ! " cried the girl ; " exactly the thing that Lucia and I have been longing for. And Rome ? Surely we shall go to Rome, father ?

Are you not glad to hear it, mother ? I am sure that we are all tired of this cold, foggy place."

The mother said nothing. If she did not exactly see the whole of the situation, she had at least an housewife's horror of a move. The poor father moved uneasily upon his chair.

" The legion will go," he said, " but your mother and you——"

" Oh, Lucius," cried the poor wife, " you do not, cannot mean that we are not to go with you ! "

" Nothing is settled," he replied, " it is true ; but I am much troubled about it. *You* might go, though I do not like the idea of your following the camp ; but these dear girls—and yet they cannot be separated from you."

The unhappy wife saw the truth only too clearly. If the times had been quiet, she might herself have possibly accompanied the legion in its march southward ; but even then she could not have taken her daughters with her, her daughters whom she never allowed to go within the precincts of the camp, except on the one day, the Emperor's birthday, when all the officers' families were expected to be present at the ceremony of saluting the Imperial likeness. And this had of late been omitted when it was difficult to say from day to day what Emperor the troops acknowledged. The centurion had spoken only too truly ; the legion might go, but they must stay behind. She covered her face with her hands and wept.

"Lucia," cried the elder girl to her sister, "we will enlist; we will take the oath; I should make just as good a soldier as many of the Briton lads they are filling up the cohorts with now; though you, I must allow, are a little too small," she added, ruefully, as she looked at her sister's plump little figure, too hopelessly feminine ever to admit the possibility of a disguise. "Cheer up, mother," she went on, "we shall find a way out of the difficulty somehow." And she threw her arms round the weeping woman, and kissed her repeatedly.

There was silence for a few minutes, broken at last by the timid, hesitating voice of the younger girl.

"But must you go, father?" she said. "Surely they don't keep soldiers in the camp for ever. And have you not served long enough? You were in the legion, I have heard you say, before even Maria was born."

"My child," said the centurion, "it is true that my time is at least on the point of being finished. Yet I can't leave the service just now. Just because I am the oldest officer the Legate counts on me, and I can't desert him. It would be almost as bad as asking for one's discharge on the eve of a battle. And besides, though I don't like troubling your young spirits with such matters, I cannot afford it.

Were I to resign now I should get no pension, or next to none. But in a year or two's time, when things are settled down, I hope to get something worth having—some post, perhaps, that would give me a chance of making a home for you."

A fifth person, who had hitherto taken no part in the conversation, and whose presence in the room had been almost forgotten by every one, now broke in, with a voice which startled the hearers by its unusual clearness and precision. Lena, mother of the centurion's wife, had nearly completed her eightieth year. Commonly, she sat in the chimney corner, unheeding, to all appearances, of the life that went on about her, and dozing away the day. In her prime, and even down to old age, she had been a woman of remarkable activity, ruling her daughter's household as despotically as in former days she had ruled her own. Then a sudden and severe illness had prostrated her, and she had seemed to shrink at once into feebleness and helplessness of mind and body. Her daughter and granddaughters tended her carefully and lovingly; but she seemed scarcely to take any notice of them. The only thing that ever seemed to rouse her attention was the sight of her son-in-law when he chanced to enter the chamber without disarming. The shine of the steel brought a fire again into her dim, sunken eyes. It was probably this that had now roused her; and her attention, once awakened, had been kept alive by what she heard.

" And at whose bidding are you going ? " she said, in a startlingly clear voice to come from one so feeble ; " this Honorius, as he calls himself, a feeble creature who has never drawn a sword in his life ! Now, if it had been his father ! He was a man to obey. He did deserve to be called Emperor. I saw him forty years ago—just after you were born, daughter—when he came with his father. A splendid young fellow he was; and one who would have his own way, too ! How he gave those turbulent Greeks at Thessalonica their deserts ! Fifteen thousand of them ! [1] That was an Emperor worth having ! "

" Oh ! mother," cried her daughter, horrified to see the old woman's ferocity, softened, she had hoped, by age and infirmity, roused again in all its old strength. " Oh ! mother, don't say such dreadful things. That was an awful crime in Theodosius, and he had to do penance for it in the church."

" Ay," muttered the old woman, " I can fancy it did not please the priests. But why," she went on, raising her voice again, " why does not Britain have an Emperor of her own ? "

---

[1] Theodosius ordered a massacre at Thessalonica on account of some offence offered to him by the populace of that city.

"So she has, mother," said the centurion. "You forget our Lord Constantine."

"Our Lord Constantine!" she repeated. "Who is Constantine? Why, I remember his mother—a slave girl—whom the Irish pirates carried off from somewhere in the North. Constantine's father bought her, and married her. Why should he be Emperor? I could make as good a one any day out of a faggot stick."

"Peace, dear mother," said the centurion, soothingly, afraid that her words might have other listeners.

"Why not you," went on the old woman, unheeding; "you are better born."

"I, Emperor!" cried the centurion. "Speak good words, dearest mother."

"Well," said the old woman, dropping her voice again, "they are poor creatures now-a-days." And she relapsed into silence, looking again as wholly indifferent to the present as if the strange outburst of rage and impatience which her family had just witnessed had never taken place.

The family discussed the position of affairs anxiously till far into the night.

"And what will happen," said the wife, "when the legions are gone?"

"There will be a British kingdom, I suppose; and, if it were united, it might stand. But it will not be united. It will be every man for him-self."

" And how about the Saxons and the Picts? If the legions hardly protected us from them, how will it be when they are gone ? "

The centurion's look grew gloomier than ever. " I know," he said, " the prospect is a sad one. But I hope that for a year you will be fairly safe ; and after that I shall hope to send for you. Or you might go over to Gaul. But I hope to see the Count of the Shore about these matters. He will give me the best advice. Here, of course, you can hardly stay, even if you cared to do it ; and some place must be found. Meanwhile, make all the prepara-tions you can for a move."

CHAPTER IX.

THE DEPARTURE OF THE LEGIONS.

THE resolution to leave Britain was announced at a general meeting of the soldiers on the following day, and was received by it with tremendous enthusiasm. To most who were present, Gaul seemed a land of promise. It was from Gaul that almost every article of luxury that they either had or wished to have was imported, and some of the necessities of life, as notably wine, were known to be both better and cheaper there than in Britain. Comfortable quarters in wealthy cities, which were ready to be friendly, or could easily be brought to reason if they were not; easy campaigns, not against naked Picts, but against civilized enemies who had something to lose; and when the time of service was over, a snug little farm, with corn land, pasture, and vineyard, and a hard-working native to till it—such were the dreams which floated through the soldiers' minds; and they were ready to go anywhere with the man who promised to make them into realities. Older and more prudent men who knew that there were two sides to the question, and the unadventurous, who were well content to stay where they were, could not resist the tide of popular feeling, and concealed, it they did not abandon, their doubts and scruples. As money was scarce, the men volunteered to forego their pay till it could be returned to them with large interest in the shape of prize-money. They even gave up to the melting pot the silver ornaments from their arms and from the trappings of their horses. The messengers who were sent with the tidings of the proposed movement to the other camps—which were now mainly to be found in the southern part of the island—found the troops everywhere well disposed, and within a few days every military station was alive with the stir and bustle of preparations for a move.

One of the most pressing cares of the new leaders of the army was the securing the means of transport. There was a great number of merchant ships, indeed, which could be pressed into the service, and which would perform it very well if only the passage in the Channel could be made without meeting opposition. The question to be considered was whether they could reckon upon this, or would the fleet, which was still supposed to acknowledge the authority of Honorius, prevent them from crossing. The chief person to be reckoned with in this matter was, of course, the Count of the Shore, and a despatch was immediately sent to him.   It was the production of Constans, and ran thus—

"*Constantine, Emperor of Britain and the West, to Lucius Ælius, Count of the Saxon Shore, greeting.*

"*Having been called to Empire by the unanimous voice of the People and Army of Britain, and desiring to give deliverance from tyranny and protection from violence to other provinces besides this my Island of Britain, I purpose to transport such forces as it may be necessary to use for this purpose to the land of Gaul.   I call upon you therefore, having full confidence in your loyalty, to give me such assistance as may be in your power, for the accomplishment of this end, and promise you, on the other hand, my favour and protection.   Farewell.*

"*Given at the Camp of the Great Harbour.*"

The Count received this communication about ten days after his arrival at the villa.   The writer would scarcely have been pleased at the comments which he made as he read it.

"'Constantine, Emperor.'   How many more Emperors are we to have in this unlucky island?   'Of Britain and the West.'   And I doubt whether he can call a foot of ground his own fifty miles from the camp.   'To deliver other provinces from oppression and violence.'   Why not begin by trying his hand at home?   'Full confidence in my loyalty.'   Truly valuable praise from so excellent a judge in the matter. 'Such assistance as may be in my power.' Well, I should be glad to see the last of this crew of adventurers and villains; but he sha'n't have my ships."

The Count's position indeed was one of singular difficulty. He had thought it best—indeed he had found it necessary, if he was to do his own work—to keep on friendly terms with the usurpers who had gone before Constantine. It had been quite hopeless for him to attempt to coerce the legions. If they chose to make Emperors for themselves, he must let them do it, so long as they did not interfere with his liberty as a loyal subject. But this was a different matter. Crossing over into Gaul meant downright hostility to the authorities in Italy. How could he help it forward? And yet how could he prevent it? He had three ships available. All the others were laid up for the winter in harbours on the eastern and south-eastern shores of the island. With these he might do some damage to the legions in their passage; but the passage he could not hope to prevent. And if he did prevent it, what would be his own future relations with the army? Clearly he could not stay in Vectis, or indeed anywhere in Britain, for there was no place which he could hope to hold against a small detachment of the army. And to go, though it could easily be done, and would save him a vast amount of trouble, would be to give up his whole work, and to leave the unhappy inhabitants of the coast without protection from the pirates of the East. After long and anxious deliberation, which he did not disdain to share with his daughter and Carna, he resolved on a middle course, by following which he would neither help nor hinder. The first thing was to seek an interview with Constantine or his representatives, and a messenger was accordingly despatched suggesting a conference to be held on shipboard, under a flag of truce, off the mouth of the Great Harbour.

The proposition was accepted, and three days afterwards the conference was held, in the way that the Count had suggested. Each party brought a single ship, which was anchored for the greater convenience of carrying on the conversation, but was perfectly ready to slip its anchor in case of any threatening of treachery. The Count's vessel had the Imperial standard at its mast-head; Constantine's, on the other hand, had no distinguishing characteristic. Both he and his two sons were present, but the father was as silent as usual, and the chief spokesman was Julian.

The Count was very brief in his greetings, and indicated, as plainly as he could without saying it in so many words, that he did not acknowledge the pretensions of the usurper.

"My lord," he said, "you have asked me to help in the transport of your army across the Channel.

Briefly then I have not the means. I have but three ships ready for sea, and not one of these can I spare."

"The Emperor can command their services," said Julian.

"I have received no instructions from my master," returned the Count, "to use them except for the protection of the coast."

"You have them now," said Julian, "and you will refuse to obey them at your peril."

"My commission is made out by Flavius Honorius Augustus, and I know no other to whom I can yield obedience."

A pause followed this plain speech; the party on board with Constantine debated the situation with some heat, Julian maintaining that the Count must be brought to reason, the others being anxious to keep on good terms with him.

"A single cohort can bring him to order," cried the young Prince.

"Can drive him out of the villa doubtless," said the more prudent Constans, "but not bring us an inch nearer getting the ships."

"We may at least count on your friendship," said Constans, Julian retiring sulkily from the negotiations; "you will not hinder the passage."

"I have nothing to do with the disposition of the legions," answered the Count, "and, as I said before, have no instructions except to defend the shore against the Pirates."

" His Majesty will not be ungrateful," said Constans.

" I owe no duty but to Honorius, and desire no favour but from him," was the Count's reply, and the conference was at an end.

The result was as favourable as Constantine could have expected. At least no opposition would be offered. Preparations for the passage were accordingly hurried on with all possible speed. All the towns along the coast were put under requisition for all the shipping that they could furnish, and, for the most part, were glad enough to answer the call. Whatever might happen in the future, it would be at least something to be rid of such troublesome neighbours. If other legions were to come, they might be more orderly and well-behaved. If these were to be the last, perhaps this would be a change for the better. Every one accordingly exerted himself to the utmost to supply the demand for transports.

It was a curious medley of vessels that assembled in the Great Harbour in the late autumn for the embarkation of the army. Old ships of war that had lain high and dry from before the memory of man were hastily pitched over and launched. Merchant vessels of every kind were there, from the huge hulks that were accustomed to carry heavy cargoes of metal from Cornwall, to the light barks that carried on the trade in wine, olive oil, fruit, and such light goods between Armorica and Britain; even the fishing vessels from the villages along the coast were pressed into the service, and laden to the full, sometimes even to a dangerous depth, with military material and all the miscellaneous property with which an army of twenty thousand men would be likely to be encumbered. The greater part of this force had been collected at the Camp of the Great Harbour, which indeed was overflowing, and more than overflowing, with troops. But the garrisons that were situated to the eastward, as at Regnum [1] and Anderida,[2] were to join the fleet as it sailed, while those from the inland and coast stations of South and Eastern Britain were to make the best of their way to the Portus Lemanus. This was to be the rendezvous for the whole force, and the point for commencing the passage. The longer voyage, direct from the Great Harbour to the mouth of the Sequana (the Seine) or the projecting peninsula, now known as Manche, was dreaded, for the Channel had even a worse reputation in those days than it has now. It was arranged, accordingly, that the flotilla should sail along the coast as far as the Portus Lemanus, and cross

---

[1] Chichester. [2] Pevensey.

from thence to Bononia.[1]   The first half of November had passed before the preparations for departure were completed, and there were some who advised Constantine to delay his passage till the following spring. That he knew to be impossible ; it was better to run any risk of storm or shipwreck than to face the winter with an ill-paid and discontented army.

At early dawn, on the fifteenth of the month, the embarkation began, the munitions of war, stores, and other baggage having been already, as far as was possible, put on board of the heavier transports. The water-gate of the camp was thrown open, and at this Constantine, his sons, and his principal officers took their place.   The priest who served the church within the camp offered a few prayers, and solemnly blessed the eagle of the Second Legion, which constituted, as has been said, the main part of the forces in the camp.   When this ceremony was concluded, Constantine addressed the army.

"By this gate in the days of our ancestors Vespasian led forth the Second Legion, then, as now, one of the chief ornaments and supports of the Empire, to execute the judgment of God on the rebellious nation of the Jews, and to receive before long as his reward the Empire of Rome.   By this gate I lead you forth, worthy successors as you are of those

---

[1] Boulogne.

who conquered with him, to a service not less honourable, and certain to receive no less distinguished a reward. Let my name, which recommended me to your favour, and this place, already famous as the starting-point of victorious armies, be accepted as omens of success. Comrades, follow me on a march which has for its end nothing less than the Capitol of Rome."

He then took his seat in a boat manned with a picked crew, and, amidst shouts of applause from the assembled soldiers and spectators, was rowed to the ship, one of the few war galleys of recent construction that were to be found in the fleet. Then began the embarkation of the troops.

It was a singular scene. The news had spread with the greatest rapidity through the whole countryside, and the native population had crowded to witness the departure. Every point from which the sight could be seen was occupied by spectators. Even the slopes of Portsdown were thickly dotted by them. Nearer the camp the emotion and excitement were intense. A regiment that marches out of a town in which it has been in garrison for a year or two leaves many sad hearts behind it; even so brief a space is long enough for the binding of many ties. But the legions had been almost permanent residents in Britain, and they were bound to its people by bonds many and close. And this people was not, it must be remembered, the self-restrained English race, so chary of sighs and groans, and so much ashamed of tears, but a race of excitable Celts, always ready to express all, and even more, than they felt. Wives, children, kinsfolk, friends were now to be left behind, and probably left for ever—for who could believe that the legions, whose departure had been threatened so long, could ever come back?

The embarkation went on. Some of the lighters could be brought close to the shore, and were boarded by gangways. To others of heavier burden the men had to be carried in boats. A strong guard had been posted to keep the place of embarkation clear. But the guard was powerless, or perhaps unwilling—for who could deal harshly with women and children so situated?—to check the rush of the excited crowd. Some of the women threw themselves on their departing husbands and lovers, clasped them round their necks, or hung to their knees. Others sat on the shore rocking themselves to and fro, or frozen by the extremity of their grief into stillness; some uttered shrill cries; others were sunk in a speechless despair. Nor were there wanting scenes of a less harrowing kind. Not a few of the departing soldiers were breaking other obligations besides those of the heart. Creditors were to be seen clinging to debtors whom they saw vanishing out of their sight. The Jew trader from the village outside the camp

THE DEPARTURE OF THE LEGIONS.

seemed to be in despair. Probably he had secured himself fairly well against the consequences of an event which he must have been shrewd enough to foresee; but to judge from the bitterness and frequency of his appeals he was hopelessly ruined. He swore by the patriarchs and prophets that he had always carried on his business at a loss, and that if his debts were not now settled in full he should be reduced to beggary. The tavern-keepers were also busy, running to and fro, getting, or trying to get, payment of scores from customers whom they had trusted. There were others who had something to sell, some provisions for the voyage, a cloak, or a mantle, and offered it as a bargain—not, however, without a margin of profit—to dear friends with whom they were not likely to have dealings again. Other noisy claimants for attention were young Britons who wanted to enlist. For days past these had been flocking into the camp, and now that their last chance was about to disappear, they became importunate in the extreme. The numbers of the legions could have been almost doubled from these candidates for service.

Slowly, as ship after ship received its complement of men, the turmoil on the shore lessened, and about sunset the embarkation was completed. The weather was beautifully calm, a light wind blowing from the land during the day, and even this falling as the

light declined. When the moon rose—the time of
the full had been chosen for the embarkation—the
sea was almost calm. Then, amidst a great cry of
" Farewell," from the shore, the fleet slowly moved
down the harbour. All night, making the most of
the favourable weather, it pursued its way along the
coast, being joined as it went by other detachments.
At the Portus Lemanus it found the fleet which
carried the garrisons of the eastern stations ready to
start, and the whole made its way without hindrance
across the Channel to Bononia, having as prosperous
a voyage as had the legions which more than four
hundred and fifty years before Cæsar had brought to
the island.

CHAPTER X.

THE winter that followed the departure of the legions
was a busy time with the Count. He was now
almost the only representative of Roman power in
Southern Britain, and the villa on the island became
a place of considerable importance. A military force
of some strength was gathered there. Constantine's
enterprise was not universally popular, and many
had taken any chance that offered itself of escaping
from it. Some had reached, or very nearly reached,
the end of their time of service, and claimed their
discharge; others were known to be loyal to Rome,
and were allowed to retire. Not a few of those who
found themselves without home or employment, and
did not happen to have friends or kinsfolk in Britain,
rallied to the Count. The families, too, of some that
had gone with the legions were glad to claim such
shelter and protection as the neighbourhood of the
villa could give. Among these were the wife and

daughters of the Centurion Decius; the old mother had steadily refused to accompany them, and, with an aged dependent of nearly the same age, continued to occupy the house near the deserted camp. It was an anxious matter with the Count what was to be done with these helpless people. While things were quiet they could live safely, if not very comfortably, in the neighbouring village; but if trouble were to come—and there were several quarters from which it might come—they would have to be sheltered somewhere in the villa. This never could be made into a really strong place; but it might serve well enough for a time and against ordinary attack. Some of the outbuildings and domestic offices were fortified as well as the position admitted; such material of war as could be got was accumulated, and provisions also were stored. The most reliable resource, however, was in the ships of war. These were not, as was usual, drawn up on the beach for the winter, but were kept at anchor, ready for immediate use.

Nor were these precautions unnecessary, for indeed, as we shall see, mischief of a very formidable kind was brewing, and indeed had been brewing ever since the departure of the legions, and even before that event. And it was mischief of a kind of which it may safely be affirmed that neither the Count nor any Roman official, had any notion. Britain, to all appearance, had for many generations been thoroughly subdued. Any Roman, if he had been told that there was any danger of rebellion among the Britons, would have laughed the suggestion to scorn. The legions, indeed, had often been mutinous and turbulent, and their generals ambitious and unscrupulous. The island indeed had gained so bad a reputation for loyalty to the Empire that it had been called the mother of tyrants, by "tyrant" being meant "usurper." But whenever Rome had been defied, she had been defied by her own troops. The Britons had enlisted in the rebel armies, but they had never attempted to assert anything like British independence. And yet the tradition of independence and liberty had always been kept alive. The Celtic race is singularly tenacious of such ideas, and also singularly skilful in concealing them from those who are its masters for the time, and the Britons were Celts of the purest blood. Caradoc[1] and Boadicea, and other heroes and heroines of British independence, were household words in many families which were yet thoroughly Roman in spirit and manners. Just as the Christianized Jews of Spain, though to all appearances devout worshippers at church, still clung in secret to the rites of their own worship, so these loyal subjects of the Empire, as all the world

---

[1] Commonly known by his Romanized name of Caractacus.

believed them, cherished in their hearts the memory of the free Britain of the past and the hope of a free Britain in the future. And the time was now at hand when their leaders thought that this hope might be fulfilled.

The Shanklin Chine of to-day is not a little different from the Shanklin Chine of fifteen hundred years ago. It has, so to speak, been subdued and civilized. Now it is a very pretty and pleasant wood ; then it was an almost impenetrable thicket, a noted lair of elk and wild boar. Inaccessible, however, as it seemed to any one who surveyed it from above, there was for those who were in the secret a way of approaching its recesses. A little path, the beginning of which it was almost impossible to discover without a guide, led up from the sea-end of the ravine to a hut which had been constructed about half way up the ascent. It consisted of a single chamber, about fourteen feet long, ten broad, and not more than seven in height, and was constructed of roughly-hewn logs, the interstices of which were filled with clay. The walls, however, were not visible, for they were covered with hangings of a dark blue material, something like serge. The floor was strewn with rushes. In the centre of the apartment there was a hearth, having over it an aperture in the roof, not, however, opening directly into the outer air, by which the smoke might escape. On this hearth two or three logs were smouldering with a dull heat which it would have been easy to fan into flame. There were two windows unglazed, but closed with rough wooden lattices.

On three settles, roughly but strongly made of oak, which, with a rudely-polished slab of wood that served for table, constituted all the furniture of the hut, sat three confederates, and behind each stood a stalwart attendant armed with a wicker shield which hung from his neck, and a long Gallic sword. The three chiefs were curiously different in appearance. One, as far, at least, as dress and manner were concerned, might have passed anywhere for a genuine Roman. He was taller, it is true, than the Romans commonly were; and his complexion, though dark rather than fair, had a ruddier hue than was often seen under the more glowing skin of Italy; still he might have walked down the Sacred Way or the Saburra [1] unnoticed save as an exceptionally handsome man, of that fair beauty which the southern nations especially admire. His hair was carefully curled and perfumed; his face as carefully shaven, and showing no trace of beard, moustache, or whisker. His oga of brilliant white, his long-sleeved tunic of some dark purple stuff, his elegant sandals, were all such as a dandy of the Palatine

---

[1] Streets of Rome.

might have worn. The one thing which would have been singular in a Roman street was the under-garment reaching to his knees, which he had assumed in consideration of the cold and wet of the insular climate. His fingers were loaded with rings, one of them a sapphire of unusual size, on which was engraved a likeness of the feeble features of the Emperor Honorius; on his left wrist might be seen a bracelet of gold.

If Martianus—for that was the name of the personage whom we have been describing—might have been easily mistaken for a Roman, the chief who sat facing him on the opposite side of the hearth was as manifestly a Briton. His hair fell over his shoulders in long natural curls which suggested no suspicion of the barber's or the perfumer's art. His upper lip was covered with a moustache which drooped to his chin. His body was covered with a sleeveless coat skilfully made of otters' skins. Both arms were bare, and were plentifully painted with woad. On his legs he wore a garment something like the "trews" or short trowsers which the Highland regiments some-times wear in lieu of the kilt; his feet were enveloped in rude boots of hide which were laced round his ankles. His ornaments were a massive chain of twisted gold, which he wore round his neck, and a single ring, rudely wrought of British gold, in which was set a British pearl of immense size but indifferent

hue.   He had a Roman name, as he could on occasion wear Roman costume, and speak the Latin tongue.   In the present company he was known and addressed by his native name of Ambiorix.

The third conspirator had the appearance of a middle-class provincial.   He wore the tunic that formed part of a Roman's ordinary dress, but not the toga, which was replaced by a garment somewhat resembling a short cloak.   But under the garb of a well-to-do townsman was concealed a very remarkable career and character.   Carausius—for this was the name by which he was generally known—was one of the last representatives of the ancient Druid priesthood.   The glory and power of this remarkable caste, which had once held itself superior to the kings of Britain, were departed.   Indeed, it was almost dangerous to hold the ancient faith, and practise the ancient worship.   Since the publication of the edict by which Constantine had made Christianity the Imperial religion, the adherents of the old religion had become fewer and feebler.   Some of the chiefs and nobles still held it in secret, or were, at least, ready to return to it, if it should ever again become powerful; but its adherents were mostly to be found among the poorer classes.   Even these in the towns were, in name at least, mostly Christians; it was only the dwellers in the remoter and wilder parts of the country that remained faithful.   But these scattered adherents revered the name of Carausius, who was believed to possess all the wisdom of his class, and was indeed credited with mysterious powers over nature and the gift of prophecy. From the Roman population all this was a secret, and the secret was remarkably well kept. Carausius was supposed to be nothing more than an ordinary farmer. His Roman neighbours would have been astonished in the last degree if they could have seen him presiding at one of the Druid ceremonies, in his white robes curiously embroidered with mystic figures, his chaplet of golden oak-leaves, and the headless spear, which was to him what the crozier was to a Christian bishop.

CHAPTER XI.

THE PRIEST'S DEMAND.

"So the time has come at last," said Ambiorix; "at last the yoke is broken from off the neck of Britain. Blessed be the day that saw the legions of the oppressor depart!"

"Yes," replied Martianus, "but will they not return? They have gone before; but have they not come back? I take it these Romans get too much out of us to let us go willingly."

"I have no fear of their return. If Honorius can make terms with this Constantine and his army, he will never send them back here; he wants them too much at home. He has got King Alaric to reckon with, and he has been long since drawing every soldier that he can from the provinces into Italy. No, depend upon it, at last Britain is free.

"Free; yes, if it has not forgotten how to move."

"We haven't all learnt to play the slave," said Ambiorix fiercely, as he started from his seat.

" There are some who have not sold their birthright for the delights of the bath and the banquet, and who are too proud to ape the manners of their masters."

" Peace, my son," interposed the aged priest; " Martianus is not the less able to help the cause of our country because he seems to be the friend of those who oppress it."

" These are but the wild words of youth, father," said Martianus. " By a wise man they are forgotten as soon as they are heard. But let us hear what Ambiorix has to tell us about the force which we can bring into the field."

The young chief entered into details which it is impossible to reproduce. Preparations had been made over nearly the whole of Britain, though the more northerly parts, owing to the perpetual attacks of their neighbours the Picts, had little to contribute in the way of help. Ambiorix knew how many men could be relied upon in every district; he was acquainted with the disposition of the representatives of the chief British families; he knew what each would want for himself, to whom he would be prepared to yield precedence, from whom he would claim precedence for himself. All his views and calculations were those of a sanguine temper; but he certainly could show—on paper at least, as we should say—a very respectable amount of strength. When he had finished his account of the resources of Britain, Martianus, who, whatever his faults, had at least a genuine admiration for ability, held out his hand—

"This is wonderful!" he said. "You have a true genius for rule. That you should keep the threads of so complicated a business all so distinct is simply wonderful. You certainly give me hopes that I never had before."

"I never doubted for a moment," returned the young man, "but that when this Roman incubus was removed all would go well. Besides, who is there to attack us? We have no enemies."

"No enemies!" replied the other, in a tone of surprise. "Do you forget the Saxons by sea and the Picts by land."

"I believe that neither will trouble us. They are not our enemies, but the enemies of Rome. They have harassed—they were quite right in harassing— the oppressors of the world : they will respect, I am sure, the liberties of a free people. When Britain is as independent as they are we shall be friends."

Martianus could not help smiling sarcastically. "That is very fine. One would think that you had been a pupil in one of the schools of rhetoric which you so much despise. The most famous of our declaimers could not have put it better. But I am afraid that there will be some difficulty in explaining all this to them."

"In any case, we can defend ourselves," returned the young chief, "though I do not think that the need will occur."

"Let us hope not," said Martianus, but his tone was not confident or cheerful.

There were, it may easily be supposed, not a few other subjects for discussion, and the conversation lasted for a long time, the young chief showing throughout such a mastery of details as greatly impressed his companions. When he had finished a brief silence followed. It was broken by the priest. There was a special solemnity in his tone, which seemed to claim an authority for his utterances, quite different from the position that he had taken up while politics or military matters were being discussed.

"My children," he said, "this is a grave matter. The weal or woe of Britain for many generations is at stake. If we fail, we may well be undone for ever. You cannot enter on so great an enterprise without the favour of the gods, and the favour of the gods is not easily to be won. For many years they have lacked the sacrifice which they most prize. I myself, though I have completed my threescore years and ten, have but once only been privileged so to honour them. The time has come for this sacrifice to be offered once more. Have I your consent, my children? But indeed I need not ask. This is a matter in which I cannot be mistaken, and from which I cannot go back."

The young chief nodded assent, but said nothing. He was evidently disturbed.

"What do you mean, father?" he said.

"The sacrifice which the gods most prize," answered the old man, "is also that which is most prized by men. The most perfect offering which we can present to them is the most perfect creature they themselves have made. Sheep and oxen may suffice for common needs; but at such a time as this, when Britain itself is at stake, we must appease the gods with the blood of MAN."

Martianus grew pale. "It is not possible," he stammered.

"Not only possible, but necessary," calmly returned the priest. "Our fathers were commonly content to offer those who had offended against the laws; but in times of special necessity they chose the noblest victims. Even our kings have given up their sons and their daughters. So it must be now."

All this was absolutely horrible to Martianus. He did not believe indeed in Christianity, but it had influenced him as it had influenced all the world. Whether he was at heart much the better may be doubted. But he was softer, more refined; he shrank from visible horrors, from open cruelty—though he could be cruelly selfish on occasion—and from bloodshed, though he would not stretch out a finger to save a neighbour's life. And what the priest said was as new and unexpected to him as it was hideous. He had no idea that this savage faith had survived in Britain.

" Father," he said, " such a thing would ruin us. Such a deed would raise the whole country against us. A human sacrifice! It is monstrous!"

" You are right so far," returned the priest, "the country must not know it. Britain is utterly corrupted by this new faith, a superstition fit only for women, and children, and slaves; and I don't doubt but that it would lift up its hands in horror at this holy solemnity. But there is no need that it should know it. It must be done secretly—so much I concede."

" And the victim?"

"Well, the days are passed when a Druid could lay his command on Britain's noblest, and be obeyed without a murmur. The victim must be taken by force, and secretly."

"And have you any such victim in your thoughts?"

The priest hesitated for a moment; but it was only for a moment. He resumed in a low voice, which it evidently cost him an effort to keep steady—

" I have not forgotten the necessity of a choice; indeed for months past it has been without ceasing in my mind, and now the choice is made. The victim whom the gods should have is a maiden, beautiful and pure. She is of noble descent, though her father was compelled, by poverty and the oppression of the Roman tyrants, to follow a humble occupation. Thus she is worthy to be offered. And yet no true Briton will regret her fate, for she has deserted the faith of her ancestors for the base superstition of the Cross."

"And her name, father?" said both of the conspirators together.

Again the priest hesitated ; a close observer might even have seen a trace of agitation in that stern countenance.

"It is Carna," he said, after a pause, which raised the suspense of his hearers almost to agony. "It is Carna, adopted daughter of Count Ælius."

And he looked steadfastly at his companions' faces, as if he would have said, "I dare you to challenge my decision."

The two started simultaneously to their feet. Not long before, young Ambiorix, who was then not yet possessed by the fanatical patriotism which now mastered him, had admired her beauty and sweetness of manner, and had had day-dreams of her as the goddess of his own hearth. Then a stronger love had come in the place of the old. It was not of woman, but of Britain free among the nations, as she had been before the restless eagles of the South had found her, that he thought day and night. Still, he could not calmly hear her doomed to a horrible death, and for a moment he was ready to rebel against the sentence of the priest.

The older man was terribly agitated. He had been for many years on the friendliest footing with the Count, a frequent guest at his table, almost an intimate of the house. And Carna was an especial favourite with him. Her sweetness, her simplicity, and a pathetic resemblance that she bore to a dead daughter of his own, touched him on the best side of his nature.

" Priest," he thundered, " it shall not be. I would sooner the whole scheme came to ruin ; I would sooner die. A curse on your hideous worship ! "

The priest had now crushed down the risings of human feelings which his training had not sufficed to eradicate.

"You have sworn by the gods," he said, "and you cannot go back. If you do not hesitate to betray Britain, at least you will not dare to betray yourself. You know the power I can command. Go back from your promise to follow my leading, and you are a dead man. You are faithful ? " he went on, turning to Ambiorix. " You do not draw back ? "

The young chief returned a muttered assent.

The older man, meanwhile, was in a miserable condition of indecision and terror. Unbeliever as he was, having long since given up the faith of his fathers, and never accepted the doctrine of the church but with the emptiest formality, he had not put from his breast the superstitious fear that commonly lingers when belief is gone. And he knew that the priest's threatened vengeance on himself was no empty boast. The strength of Druidism had passed, but it still had fanatics at its command, whose daggers would find their way sooner or later to his heart. The cold, cynical look with which he had entered on the conference had given place to mingled looks of rage, remorse, and fear.

"You must have your own way," he muttered, sullenly.

"My son," said the priest, in a tone which he made studiously cautious, "what is one life in comparison with the happiness and glory of our nation? You, I know, would shrink from no sacrifice, and, believe me," he added in a lower voice, for he had to play off the two rivals against each other, "believe me, whatever sacrifice you make shall not miss its reward."

CHAPTER XII.

LOST.

CARNA was known all over the neighbourhood of the villa as the best and kindest of nurses, always ready to help in cases of sickness, and able to command the services of the household physician where her own medical skill was at fault. It was therefore with no surprise that the morning after the consultation, recorded in the last chapter, she was told that her help was wanted in a case of urgent need. The woman who had brought the message was a stranger. She was the daughter, she said, of an old woman living at Uricum, a small hamlet about four miles from the villa. She had happened to come the day before on a visit to her mother, and found her very ill; they had no medicines in the house, and indeed should not have known how to use them if they had. Would the lady come, and, if she thought proper, bring the physician with her ? The place mentioned was on the limits of the district with which Carna was acquainted. It could only be approached by a path through the forest; and the girl had not visited it more than two or three times in her life. She had a vague remembrance, however, of the patient's name. On sending for the physician, it was found that he was out, having been called away, Carna was told, to a case which, he had said before starting, would probably occupy him for the greater part of the day. On hearing this, she made up her mind to start without waiting for him. The illness was very probably of a simple kind, though it might be violent in degree. Very likely it was a case in which the nurse would be more wanted than the doctor. She provided herself with two or three simple remedies which she learnt to employ in the ordinary maladies of the country, of which feverish colds were the most common, and started, taking with her as companion and protector a stately Milesian dog, or mastiff, who was always delighted to play the part of a guard in her country walks. Her own pet dog, a long-haired little creature, something of the Spanish kind, whom she had intended to leave at home, contrived to free himself from the custody to which he had been assigned, and stealthily followed her, cunningly keeping out of sight till the party had gone too far for him to be conveniently sent back. He then showed himself with extravagant gestures of contrition, was tenderly reproached, pardoned, and allowed to go on.

During the walk the messenger was curiously silent, and answered all Carna's questions about her mother and her affairs in the very briefest fashion. All that could be got from her was that she lived on the main land, about twenty miles inland, in a northerly direction, and that since her marriage, now twenty years ago, she had seen very little of her mother. When they reached the outskirts of the hamlet she pointed out her mother's house, and, making an excuse that she had an errand for a neighbour, disappeared. Carna, seeing nothing but a certain surliness of temper, possibly only shyness, in her companion, went on without suspicion. She reached the house, and knocked at the door. There was no answer. She knocked again. Still all was silence. Looking a little more closely at the place she could see no signs of habitation, no smoke, for instance, making its way out of the thatch (for chimneys did not yet exist, at least, in the poorer dwellings). The next thing was to peep in at the window, a wooden lattice, which had been left partially open. The room into which she looked was perfectly bare.

A suspicion rushed into her mind that she had been tricked, and that danger of some unknown kind was at hand. The strange sympathy which often makes the dog so quick to understand the feelings of man, made the big mastiff, Malcho, uneasy. With a low growl, showing uneasiness rather than fear or anger, he ranged himself at her side.

As she stood considering what was next to be done, a party of six men, one of whom led a horse, issued from the wood which bordered the little garden of the cottage.

" Can you tell me where I shall find one Utta, who, I am told, is sick, and wishful to see me ? Can it be that I have mistaken the house ? "

" Utta, my lady," said one of the party, " is not to be found any more. She died a week since."

" But," said Carna, with rising anger, " a woman, who said that she was her daughter, told me, not more than two hours ago, that she was sick, and desired to see me. Why have I been brought here for nothing ? "

" Pardon me, lady," returned the first speaker, in a tone in which respect and command were curiously blended, " but you have not been brought for nothing. You have a better work to do than ministering to a sick old woman."

As he spoke he moved forwards. But he had not taken two steps before the great dog, who had been watching the speakers, we might say almost listening to their talk with the most eager attention, sprang furiously at him, and laid him prostrate on the ground.

His companions rushed to rescue their leader from the dog and to seize the girl. They did not accomplish either of their objects with impunity. The gallant creature turned from one assailant to another with a strength and a fury which made him a most formidable antagonist, and he had inflicted some frightful wounds before he was made senseless by repeated blows from the weapons of the assailants. Nor was Carna overpowered without a struggle. Weapons she had none, except a little dagger, meant for use in needlework, which hung at her side; but she used this not without effect. She clenched her fist, and dealt two or three blows, of which her antagonists bore the marks upon their faces for days to come. Finally she wrenched herself from the grasp of the assailants as a last resource, and endeavoured to fly, but it was a hopeless effort. Before she had run more than a few yards she was overtaken. Her captors used no more violence than they could help. Probably had they been less unwilling to hurt her, she could not have resisted so long. Finding her so strong and so determined, they were obliged to bind her hands and feet; but they did this with all the gentleness compatible with an evident resolve to make her bonds secure. In the midst of her terror and distress Carna could not help observing with astonishment that the cords which they used were of silk. Then finding herself absolutely helpless, she said—

THE CAPTURE OF CARNA.

" Do not bind me as though I were a slave. On the faith of a Christian, I will not attempt to escape."

" Lady, we trust you," said the leader of the party, and at the same time directed one of his companions to unbind the ropes. " Be comforted," he went on ; " we do not intend you harm ; on the contrary, high honour is in store for you."

Carna was scarcely reassured by these mysterious words, but she had now recovered her calmness. Summoning up all her courage — and it was far beyond even the average of a singularly fearless race —she intimated to her captors that she was ready to follow them without further delay. They mounted her upon the horse, which, as has been said, one of them was holding, and started in a northerly direction. Two of the party had been so severely injured by the hound, that they were obliged to stay behind. One of the others held the bridle of the horse, and led him forward at an ambling pace ; the others followed behind.

The way of the party lay entirely along rough forest-paths which seemed from their appearance, often grown over as they were with branches and creepers, to be but seldom traversed. Night had fallen some hours before they reached the northern coast of the island. Their way had lain in a north-westerly direction, and they emerged near to the arm of the sea now known as Fishbourne Creek. Here they found a rowing boat in waiting.

Carna's captors now handed over their charge to the boat party, which was under the command of the young chief whom we know by the name of Ambiorix. He received his prisoner with a dignified civility, made her as comfortable as he could with rugs and wraps in the stern of the boat, and then gave orders to start. The journey across the channel, which we now know as the Solent, occupied some hours, though the night was calm, and the ebbing tide mostly in the rowers' favour, the shortest route not being taken, but a north-westerly direction still followed. The morning was just beginning to break when the coast was reached near the spot where Lymington now stands. The party hurriedly disembarked, put the girl on a rough litter which they had with them in the boat, and carried her to a dwelling some half-mile inland, and surrounded by the woods which here almost touched high-water mark. Carna found a tolerable chamber allotted to her, where she was waited upon by an elderly woman who seemed bent on doing everything that she could for her comfort. The girl was of the elastic temper which soon recovers itself even under the most depressing circumstances. She had the wisdom, too, to feel that, if she was to help herself, she must keep up her strength to the very best of her power. She did not refuse the simple but well-cooked meal which her attendant served to her, after she had enjoyed the refreshment of a bath. And then over-powered by the fatigue of a journey which had lasted not much less than twenty-four hours, she sank into a deep sleep.

It was dark when her attendant gently roused her and told her that in an hour she would be required to resume her journey, in which, as Carna heard with some pleasure, she was herself to be her com-panion. A start was made about three hours before midnight, and the journey was continued till an hour before dawn. This plan was followed till their destination was reached. The party was evidently careful to keep its movements secret. Their way lay as before, by woodland paths, leading them through the district now known as the New Forest. They travelled but slowly, more slowly indeed than they had done on the island, for the paths were still rougher, and, in fact, almost undistinguishable. Carna, too, was the only one of the company that had a horse, and her female attendant, who was neither young nor active, could manage but a few miles at a time. It was the morning of the second day after they had left the coast before they reached the edge of the great forest known as the Natanleah. Some five miles to the west lay Sorbiodunum, now Salisbury. This was a Roman town of some importance, and had of course to be avoided by the party, who, indeed, were anxious, as Carna could gather from a few scattered words that were let drop in her presence, as to the way in which the rest of their journey was to be accomplished. The country was open, cultivated, and comparatively populous, the inhabitants being, for the most part, thoroughly Latinized. Two Roman roads, too, had to be crossed before their destination was reached.

The day was spent as usual in concealment and repose. An hour after nightfall the party started. They had now managed to procure another horse for Carna's attendant; and as the ground was fairly level, unenclosed, and, at that time of year, unencumbered by crops, they moved rapidly onwards. The moon had now risen, and Carna, for the first time, could at least see where they were going. She was still, however, at a loss to know what part of the country they had reached. At midnight a halt was called, and the leader of the party proceeded to blindfold the captive's eyes. But if he wanted to keep her in ignorance of the locality, he was a little too late. The girl's quick sight had caught a glimpse in the distance of the huge circle of earth walls, now known as Amesbury. She had never seen the place, but it was known to her in the chronicles of her people. There, as she had read with a patriotism which all her Roman surroundings had not been able to quench, her countrymen had more than once held at bay the legions of Rome. She knew roughly the situation of the famous camp of the Belgæ, and she was sure that these massive fortifications, just seen for a moment in the moonlight, could be none others than those of which she had read so often.

When the bandage was removed, she found herself in a chamber larger and more comfortably furnished than any she had hitherto occupied on her journey. Part of the palace of one of the old kings of the Belgæ was still standing, and the travellers had taken up their quarters in it. The Amesbury camp was indeed as safe a place as they could have chosen. It was a spot which no Roman, much less a Briton living under Roman protection, would care to visit. The whole countryside believed that it was haunted by the spirits of the great chiefs and warriors who had been buried within its precincts, and of the slaves who had been killed to furnish them with service and attendance in the unseen world. The scanty remnant who still clung to the Druid faith found their account in encouraging these superstitions. More than one appearance had been arranged to terrify sceptical or curious persons who had been rash enough to visit the vast circle of embankments. For many years before the time of our story the enclosure had been untrodden except by the few who were in the secret of the Druid

initiation.   Here, then, the party waited securely
with their prisoner till the time should come for the
solemn visit to *Choir Gawr*, the Great Temple,
known to us by the name of Stonehenge.

CHAPTER XIII.

WHAT DOES IT MEAN?

IT was some time before the prolonged absence of Carna caused any alarm at the villa. When she was on one of her errands of kindness among the sick, it was difficult to say when she would return. But in the course of the afternoon the old physician returned, not a little wrath that he had been sent on a fool's errand. He had been told that an old farmer, living close to the north-west of the island some seven or eight miles from the villa was lying dangerously ill, and he had found the supposed patient in vigorous health, and not a little angry at being supposed to be anything else. This seemed to make things look somewhat serious. It was easy to guess that the trick played upon the physician had something to do with the message brought to Carna. It was remembered that the stranger had asked that he should accompany the girl; it was at least possible that she knew him to be out of the way, and that she would not have made the request had she not known it.

While the Count, who had just returned from an inspection of his crews, was talking the matter over with his daughter and two of his officers who happened to be present, a new cause for suspicion and alarm presented itself. Carna's pet dog had found its way back with a bit of broken cord round its neck, and refused to be comforted, tearing and pulling at the dresses of the attendant, and saying, as plainly as a dog could say it, that there was something wrong, that it must be attended to at once, and that he would show them how to do it, if they would only follow him. When the rope round his neck was examined more closely, it was found that it had been gnawed in two. "He has been tied up and has broken away," said the Count, when this was pointed out to him. "And if I know the dear little thing," broke in Ælia, "he would not have left his mistress as long as he could be near her. I am sure that some mischief has happened to her." And this was the general impression, though, who could have ventured on so audacious an outrage it was impossible to guess.

What had happened, as the reader may possibly guess, was this. The dog had remained with Carna, showing his love, not by fierce resistance like that made by his powerful companion, for which he had the sagacity to know he had not sufficient strength, but by keeping as close to her as he could. After she had been made a prisoner, and while the party were preparing for a start, he had been tied to a tree. It had been intended that he should go with his mistress, for whom, as has been said, her captors showed throughout a certain consideration, but it so happened that in the bustle of departure he was forgotten. When he saw her go and found himself left behind, he set himself with all his might to gnaw the rope which fastened him to the tree. This task took him a long time, for he was an old dog, and his teeth were not as good as they had been. Finding himself free he started in headlong pursuit, easily tracking the party by the scent, but after a while he halted; a happy thought—is it possible that, in the teeth of all accumulated evidences, any one can deny that dogs can think?—a happy *thought* then struck his mind, quickened to its utmost capacity of intelligence by love and grief. We may translate it into human language thus: " If I follow her and overtake her, what good can I do? but if I go back and make the people at home understand that something has happened to her, then I can help her to some purpose." This was his conclusion, anyhow. How he arrived at it only He knows who makes all things great and small, and " divideth to all severally as He will." He turned back, ran with breathless speed to the villa, and did all that could be done, short of speaking, to show that his dear mistress was in trouble.

Meanwhile, however, much time had been lost, and the day was already far advanced. Anxious as was the Count to set out, he could not but perceive that haste might defeat the object of his journey. To start when the light was failing would probably be to miss important signs of what had happened, and, very possibly, to risk success. All preparations, however, were made. The men who were to form the pursuing party were chosen. As it may be supposed, there was no lack of volunteers. There was not a single being at the villa or its dependencies that would not have given a great deal and borne a great deal to see Carna again in safety. But it would be possible to take only a small number, if the pursuit was to be rapid and effective. Some of the most active of the crews of the war-ships accordingly were chosen, sailors having then as now a cheerful activity that makes them particularly valuable members of a land expedition. The Count added others from his own establishment, and he determined to conduct the party himself. It was arranged that it should start the following day, as soon as it should be sufficiently light.

One of the slaves who was early astir on the following morning found fixed to an outside gate of the villa a document, rudely written and roughly folded, which bore the Count's address. It was found, when opened, to contain the following message, expressed in ungrammatical Latin, mingled with one or two British words:

"*She whom you seek is not far off, and may be recovered by you if you are wise. If you attempt to regain her by force, she will be lost to you altogether. But if you wish to have her again with you safely and without trouble, send one whom you can trust with a hundred gold pieces at midnight three days after the receiving of this letter to the place to which she was yesterday fetched. Let your messenger go alone, and ask no questions then or afterwards.*"

"So she is held to ransom by a set of brigands," cried the Count, when he had read this document. "I should not have thought that such a thing had been possible in Britain. But the times have been getting worse and worse. We have. long been weakening our hold upon the province, and we had better clear out altogether, if we cannot do better than this. But I suppose we have no choice. We must not endanger the dear girl's life. But now the question is about the money. I do not think that I have so much in gold in the house; but we can borrow somewhere what is wanted.

"Perhaps," said the Count's secretary, whom he had summoned to consult with him, "the peddler can help you. He has the reputation of being richer than he looks."

"Well," replied the Count, "that would be a simple way out of the difficulty, if it can be managed. Meanwhile, let me see what I have got of my own at hand."

It was found that eighty gold pieces were forthcoming, and the peddler was summoned and asked whether he could make up the balance.

"My Lord," said the man when he was brought into the Count's presence and had heard the story, "I will make no idle pretence of poverty. I have what you want, and it is entirely at your lordship's service. But will you let me see the letter in which this demand for ransom is made?"

The Count handed him the document, and he examined it long and carefully.

"My lord," he said, "the more I look at this, the more I am confirmed in certain suspicions which have been growing up in my mind. I have been thinking of this matter, and of other matters which seem to me to be connected with it all the night. It will take long to explain, and, of course, after all I may be wrong; still, I think you would do well to hear what I have got to say."

The Count, who had previously had reasons for

thinking well of the peddler's intelligence, bade him proceed.

"In the first place," continued the man, "I think this letter is a blind. It is made to look like the work of some very rude and ignorant person. But the pretence is not well kept up. You will see, if you look at the handwriting a little more closely, that it is feigned. The writer was perfectly able to make it a great deal better than it is, if he had so chosen, and he has sometimes forgotten his part. Some of the letters, some even of the words, particularly of the small words, about which he would naturally be less careful, are quite well-formed. Now a really bad writer, I mean one who writes badly because he does not know how to write well, is always bad; every letter he forms is mis-shapen."

The Count examined the document and acknowledged that this comment upon it was just. And he began to see too what was naturally more apparent to him, as an educated man, than it was to the peddler, that the style was hardly what would have been expected from an ignorant scribe.

"What, then, is your conclusion?" he asked.

"About that," returned the other, "I am not so certain. That this is a blind, as I said, I am sure; and this talk about the ransom consequently is a deception. 'Three days,' you see it says. That would be three days lost.   No, my lord, it is not by robbers that this has been planned."

"What then?" cried the Count, flushing a fiery red as a sudden thought occurred to him.   "Carna is very beautiful.   Do you think——"

"No," said the peddler, "I think not.   A lover would not lay so elaborate a plot as I fancy I can see here.   I think the Lady Carna is a hostage, or——"

He paused, and continued after a few minutes of silence.   "I have much to piece together, and it would take long, and lose much precious time.   That is the last thing that we should do.   They have got too much start already.   We must not let them improve it more than we can help.   You will let me go with you, and I shall have leisure to put all I have got to say together without hindering you. But the sooner we are on their track the better."

To this the Count readily agreed, and preparations for immediate departure were made.   It was with difficulty that Ælia could be persuaded that she must be left behind.   But when it was pointed out to her that her presence must inevitably make the progress of the party more slow, and increase their anxieties, she reluctantly gave way.   At the last moment an unexpected addition was made to the party in the person of the Saxon prisoner.

"My lord," said the peddler, to whom the young

man had communicated his earnest desire to be allowed to go; "it may seem a strange thing for me to say, but you cannot have a better helper in this matter than this young fellow. He is as strong as any horse, and as keen and intelligent a youth as I ever saw. And in this case too his wits will be doubly sharp, and his arm doubly strong, for he worships the very ground that the Lady Carna treads upon."

"Very well," replied the Count, with a smile, "let him go. After all, it is quite as safe to take a lion about with one, as to leave him at home."

The pet dog was, of course, a valued member of the expedition.

CHAPTER XIV.

THE PURSUIT.

THE task of tracing the lost girl was at first easy enough. She and the stranger, who, it now seemed, had been sent to entrap her, had been seen proceeding in the direction mentioned in the message. The neighbourhood of the villa was mostly cultivated ground, and there had been people at work in the fields who had noticed the girl's well-known figure. Beyond this belt of cultivated country, which might have been about a mile broad, there was only one road which it was possible for her to have taken. Following this, and reaching the hamlet at the further end of which, as we have seen, the abduction had taken place, they still found themselves on the right track. A child had seen two people, one of them, she said, a pretty lady, pass by on the morning of the day before. The lady had smiled, and said a few words to her in her own language, and had given her a sweetmeat. Further on the traces of what they were looking for became still more evident. There were marks of struggle on the ground, for Carna, as we have seen, had not suffered herself to be taken without resistance; a button was found on the ground, which the peddler at once identified as one of his own selling. And a little off the path, the tree was found to which the dog had been tied, with the fragment of string still attached to it. Curiously enough, no traces of the great dog could be found.

Nor did the next step in the pursuit delay them long. There were, it is true, three paths through the forest, which closed in the hamlet on every side except that by which the party had approached it. Carna's pet dog at once decided for the searchers which of the three they should follow. He discovered the scent very quickly, ran at the top of his speed along the path thus distinguished from the others for about a hundred yards, and then, coming back, implored the party, so to speak, by his gestures, that they should come with him. It was evident that the path had been traversed by a party of considerable size, whose tracks, the marks of a horse's hoofs among them, were still fresh in the ground, soft as it was with the winter rains. The dog was evidently satisfied that they were right, for he ran quietly on, now and then giving a very soft little whine. It wanted still an hour or so of sunset when the party emerged out of the forest upon the shore.

Here it might have seemed at first all trace was lost. The tide had flowed and ebbed twice since the girl had been there, and had swept away all marks of footsteps. The dog too was no longer a guide. The poor little creature's distress indeed was pitiful, as he ran to and fro upon the shore with a plaintive whine.

The Count asked his companions for their opinions.

"Have they taken to the wood again, do you think? or have they crossed the water? they may have gone a mile or more along the shore and then entered the forest. In that case it seems hopeless to recover the track."

"It is my opinion," said the peddler, "that they have crossed to the mainland; but it is only an opinion, and I have little or nothing to urge for it."

Other members of the party had different views; and, on the whole, opinion was adverse to the peddler's view; and the Count was about to order a search in the direction of the wood further along the shore, when the attention of the party was arrested by a shout from the Saxon.

The discussion had been carried on in a language which he had still some difficulty in understanding, and he had been pacing backwards and forwards along the shore, seemingly lost in thought, but really watching everything with that keen attention to all outward objects which is one of the characteristics of uncivilized man. It was thus that something caught his eye. He plunged his hand into one of the little rock-pools upon the shore, and drew it out. It was a small gold trinket, which the girl had dropped in the forlorn hope that it might be found. Its weight, for it was an almost solid piece of metal, had kept it in the place where it fell, and as the night and day had been uniformly calm, there had been no sufficient movement of the water to disturb it. With a cry of delight the Saxon held it up, and the Count recognized it at once.

" Ah ! " said the peddler, " I knew the fellow would be of use to us. If the Lady Carna is anywhere on the earth he would find her. This proves, my lord, that they have crossed the sea. They would certainly have not come down so far from the shore as this."

This seemed too probable to admit of any doubt. Happily it had occurred to the Count that it would be well to have some kind of vessel at his command, and he had ordered a pinnace to start from the haven as soon as it could be got ready, and to coast along the shore of the island, watching for any signal that might be given. The land party had outstripped the ship, which, indeed, had not started till somewhat later. Still, it might be expected very soon. Meanwhile there was an opportunity for discussing the aspect which the affair now bore.

After various opinions had been given, the Count

turned to the peddler. "And what do you think of the affair ? "

" I have a notion," the man replied, "but it may be only a fancy—still I seem to myself to have a notion of what their purpose is."

" Do you mean," pursued the Count, as the other paused, and seemed almost unwilling to speak, " do you mean that they think of holding her as a kind of hostage against me ?   Do they fancy that I shall not be able to act against them, and shall hinder my colleagues from acting, as long as she is in their power ? or will they keep her as something to make terms about if they fail ? "

The other was still silent for a few minutes, and seemed to be collecting his thoughts.   At last he said :

" My lord, what I am going to tell you may seem as foolish as a dream. I should have gone on saying nothing about it, as I have said nothing about it hitherto, if things had not happened which makes it a crime for me to be silent any longer. You find it difficult to believe that a rebellion is possible among a nation which you have always looked upon as thoroughly subdued. But what will you say if I tell you that this rebellion has been preparing for generations, and that the Druids have been, and are, at the bottom of it."

" Druids ! " cried the Count, " I did not know

that there were any Druids.   I thought that the last
of them had disappeared years ago."

"Not so," replied the peddler ; "the people who
rule do not know what is going on about them. Now
I have been among this people the greater part of
my life.   I have seen them, not as they show themselves to you, but as they are.   You think that they
are Christians—not very good Christians, perhaps,
but still not worse than other people—and believing
the Creeds, if they believe anything.   Now I know
for a certainty that many of them are no more
Christians now than their fathers were three hundred
and fifty years ago.   I have seen sometimes, when
no one knew that I saw, what they really worshipped.
I have pieced together many little things.   I have
heard hints dropped unawares, and I know that
there is a secret society, which has existed ever since
the island was conquered, which has for its object
the bringing back of the old faith.   I could name—
if things turn out as I expect they will, I will name—
men whom you believe to be quiet, respectable
citizens, but who are the heads of a conspiracy
reaching all over Britain, against Rome and the
Christian Church.   You never see them except in
the tunic and the cap, but they can wear on occasion
the Druid's robe and crown."

"But tell me," said the Count, with a certain impatience, "what has this got to do with my
daughter?"

"This, my lord," answered the other, "that if the Druids are making the great effort for which they have been preparing for no one knows how many years, they will begin it with all the solemnity that is possible—in a word, with the great sacrifice. This, I suppose, has not been practised for many generations, but it has not been forgotten. To speak plainly, I believe that the Lady Carna has been carried off for the victim."

The Count staggered back as if he had been struck. "Impossible!" he cried. "Such things cannot be in Britain: and why should they fix upon her?"

"For two reasons," said the peddler. "She is of royal race. You very likely do not know or care about such things. All Britons to you will be much about the same; but they do not forget it. Yes, though her father was nothing more than a sailor, she is descended from Cassibelan. And then she is a Christian. These are the two reasons why they have chosen her—this is what they honour her for, and this is what they hate her for."

"But where," cried the Count, "where is this monstrous thing to be done?"

"That," replied the other, "I think I know. It can hardly be done anywhere but at the Great Temple, the Choir Gawr, as they call it themselves."

"And where is this Great Temple?"

"About forty miles inland, in a nearly northerly direction. I have seen the place once, and I can find my way to it, I believe; but, to make sure, I will find a guide."

"And when?"

"At the full moon, I should say."

"And how much does it want to the full moon now?"

"It will be full moon to-morrow night."

"We have to cross then to the mainland—and the galley is not in sight—to find a guide, and to travel forty miles, and all before to-morrow night. Well, it must be done. To think of these wretches murdering my dear Carna!"

"Do not fear, my lord; we shall do it," said the peddler; but added, in a low voice, "if nothing happens."

At that moment the galley came in sight. "That is right," cried the Count; "anyhow, we begin well; no time will be lost in getting across."

CHAPTER XV.

THE PURSUIT (*continued*).

THE signal previously agreed was promptly hoisted by the party on shore, and as promptly observed and obeyed by the crew of the galley which had been for some time on the watch for some communication.

" My lord," said the peddler, when they had embarked, " if I may suggest, we should not make a straight passage to the mainland from here, but steer for the north-west. Some eight miles beyond the western point of the island there is a river flowing into the sea, and a fishing village at the mouth. I know the place well, and have one or two good friends there. We shall get a guide there; I have in my mind the very man who will suit us well in that capacity. Indeed the river [1] itself would be no bad guide. The Great Temple lies but a few miles westward from its upper course. The road will be easy too along the valley, which is mostly clear of wood."

---

[1] This river, of course, must have been the Avon.

" Then," said the Count, " the Temple cannot be far from Sorbiodunum.   Why not make for the Great Harbour, and go by the Great Road to Venta [1] and from Venta to Sorbiodunum.[2]   The travelling would be much easier."

" I have thought of that," said the other, " but I think my plan the best.   The distance is far less, and, what is quite as important, we shall not be expected to come that way.   Depend upon it there will be an ambuscade laid somewhere along the road; for they will feel sure that we shall try and come that way."

It was evident anyhow that as far as the sea voyage was concerned the man was right.   The tide was ebbing slowly, and an east wind, already high and still rising, was blowing.   To make way against wind and tide to the Great Harbour would be in any case a laborious business; and if the wind increased to a gale as it threatened to do, might become impossible. The galley had been chosen for swiftness rather than seaworthy qualities in rough weather, and might fail in the attempt to work back.   On the other hand both wind and tide thoroughly favoured a westward voyage.

Indeed she moved gaily on with a strong breeze, that in the phraseology of to-day would be called a half-gale, blowing due aft, and scarcely felt the heavy

---

[1] Winchester.   [2] Salisbury.

sea, seeming to leave the waves behind, as the rowers bent their backs to their work. The Saxon had now taken his place on one of the thwarts, and his gigantic strength, put it was evident with a will into the labour, seemed of itself to drive the galley forwards. In an incredibly short time the river mouth was reached, the galley stranded, and the guide, who, by great good luck, had just returned from a fishing voyage, engaged.

But now an unforeseen obstacle opposed itself. A few specks of rain had been felt by the party as they went, and then as the day went on, began to change to snow. And now the wind almost suddenly died away, and at the same time the fall of snow grew heavier. The face of the guide fell.

" My lord," he said, " I hear that your business is urgent and cannot wait. But I must tell you that the weather looks very bad, and that the prospects of our journey are almost as unfavourable as they can be. We shall have a very heavy fall of snow, and if the wind gets up again, and it begins to drift, we shall be blocked, and possibly unable to get either backwards or forwards."

" We must go," said the Count, in a determined voice, " though the snow were over our heads."

After a very short interval allowed for refreshment, the party started. At first the snow was no very serious obstacle; but after a couple of hours incessant and rapid fall, it began to make movement very difficult. The progress of the travellers grew slower and slower, and the Count began to calculate that at their present rate of speed they could but barely arrive in time. It was an immense relief when the sky almost suddenly cleared, and showed the moon still evidently somewhat short of the full. But the relief was only temporary. The clearer weather was the result of a change of wind, which had suddenly veered to a point westward of north and which was rapidly increasing in force. And now occurred the thing which the peddler's knowledge of the country and the weather had suggested to him—the snow began to drift. At first the party was hardly conscious of the change; indeed for a time the way was somewhat clearer and easier than before; then as they came to a slight depression, the snow was felt to be certainly deeper. Still three or four miles were traversed without any particular difficulty. Then the leader of the party suddenly plunged into a drift considerably above his knees. This obstacle, however, was surmounted, or rather avoided by making a *détour.* But still the wind rose higher and higher, and as it rose, not only did its force hinder the party's advance, but the drifts grew now formidably deep. Some of the party began to lag behind; the Count himself, who was past his prime, began to acknowledge to himself, with an agony of anger and fear in his heart, that his strength was failing. Still they struggled on, leaving one or two of the strugglers to make the best of their way back, or, it might well be, to perish in the snow, till about half the distance was traversed. They had now reached a little hamlet,[1] on the outskirts of which there happened to be a small villa. It was shut up, the proprietor chancing to be absent, but it was put at the disposal of the party by the person who was in charge. Fires were hastily lighted, and the travellers, most of whom had almost reached the end of their powers of endurance, were refreshed with warmth and food.

The Count held a council of war. The situation indeed eemed nothing less than desperate. Two out of the party of twenty-five—their numbers had been increased by a contingent taken from the crew of the galley—were missing. They had fallen out on the march, and it was too probable that they had perished in the snow. Of the remainder but four or five seemed fit for any further exertion. By far the freshest and most vigorous of them was the Saxon. The fatigues of the night had scarcely told on his gigantic strength. The Italians, and even the Britons, natives of the southern parts of the island, and little accustomed to heavy falls of snow, looked at him

---

[1] Now known as Downton, a small market town, about five miles south of Salisbury.

with astonishment. As for him, he was full of impatience at the delay.

The Count was in an agony of doubt and distress. His own strength had failed so completely that all his spirit—and there was no braver man in the armies of Rome—could not have dragged him a hundred yards further. And he saw that many of his followers were in little better case. And yet to give up the pursuit! to leave Carna, the sweetest, gentlest of women, dear to him as a daughter of his own, to this hideous death! The thought was too dreadful.

" When do they perform their horrible rites ? " said the Count to the peddler.

" When the full moon shines through the great south entrance of the Temple," was the answer.

" And when will that be ? "

" To-night, and about an hour before midnight, as far as I can guess."

" And what must be done ? What is your advice?"

" There seems to me only one thing possible. Those who can must press on. I count a greal deal on the Saxon. His strength and endurance are such as I never saw in any man, and they now seem to be increased manyfold. Anything that can be done by mortal man, he, you may be sure, will do. Our guide too has happily something still left in him ; and there are three or four others who are equal to going on after they have had a little rest. I should say, let them get two or three hours' sleep, and then push on to Sorbiodunum. That is not far from here, and they can easily reach it before noon to-day, after allowing a fair time for rest. Perhaps they may get some help there, though the place is not what it was. It is some years since I paid it a visit, and then I found it in a very declining condition, so much so that it was not worth my while to go there again. There were not more than two or three Roman traders there, and they made but a very poor living out of their business."

This seemed to be the best course practicable under the circumstances. The Saxon, with whom the peddler held a long conversation, was for pressing on at once, and would almost have gone alone, but for want of a guide. When he understood the state of the case he yielded to what he perceived to be a necessity, and throwing himself down on the hearth was almost immediately buried in a profound sleep, an example which was soon followed by the rest of the party, the Count and the peddler excepted.

Not more than two hours could be allowed for rest. The guide and the three sailors who had volunteered to go on were roused with no little difficulty; the young Saxon was wide awake in a moment. The party partook hastily of a meal of bread, meat, and hot wine and water, which the peddler had been busying himself in preparing while they slept, and, after stowing away some provisions for the day, started on their journey about two hours before noon.

Sorbiodunum was reached without much difficulty. But there a great disappointment awaited them. The peddler's anticipations were more than fulfilled, for the town was almost deserted. Only one Roman remained there. He was an old man who had married a British wife, and who cultivated a farm which had descended to her from her father. When the guide handed to him the letter which the Count had addressed to the authorities of the town, begging for any help which they could give in saving the liberty and life of a person very dear to himself, he shook his head. When he heard the whole of the guide's story, he became still more depressed.

" Authorities ! " he said, " there are no authorities. I am the only Roman left in the place, and I do not know where to look for a single man to help you. As for the Great Temple on the plain there is not a creature here who would dare to go near it. They think it haunted by spirits and demons. And indeed there *are* strange stories about it. To tell you the plain truth, I should not much care to go there my-self. No ; I see nothing to be done. But I will ask my wife. Perhaps her woman's wit will help us."

Bidding the party be seated, he left the room in which he had received them, and entered the kitchen, where his wife was busy with her domestic affairs.

In about half an hour he returned.   His expression was now a shade more cheerful than before.

"Ah!" he said, "I was right about the woman's wit.   She *has* thought of something.   You must know that my wife is a very devout Christian—for myself I am a Christian too, but I must own that I don't see so much in it as she does—and that she has brought up our children in that way of thinking.   Now, our eldest son is a priest in a village some seven miles hence, and his people are devoted to him.   If there is any one in this neighbourhood who can give you the help you want it is he.   He has only got to say the word and his people will follow him to the end of the world.   Here is a proof of it.   Four years ago a strong party of Picts came this way, ravaging and plundering wherever they went.   There were not more than fifty of them, but the people were as terrified as if they were so many demons.   If you think this place a desert now, what would you have thought it then?   There was not a single person left in it—at least a single person that could help himself—for the cowards had the meanness to leave some of the old and the sick behind them.   But my son was not going to let the robbers have it all their own way—you know he has something of the Roman in him—and he went about talking to his people in such a way, that they plucked up spirit, and fell on the Picts one night when they were expecting nothing less than an attack, and gave such an account of them, that the country has not been troubled since with the like of them. Well, as I say, he is the man to help you. I have my younger son here working with me on the farm; he is just such another as his elder brother, and would have been a priest too if he had not felt it to be his duty to stay and help me. I will bring him in, and he shall hear the whole story and carry it to his brother. That is the best hope that I can give you, and I really think that it is worth something. What I can do for you does not go beyond hospitality, but to that you are heartily welcome. You have some hours before you. If you start an hour after sunset you will be in ample time. And, in fact, you had better not start before, because the less that is seen of your movements the better. I don't know that any of the people about here are infected with the Druid superstition, though I have had one or two hints to that effect, hints which what you have just told me helps to explain. But, in any case, the more secret you are the better. Besides, my son's Party cannot reach the Great Temple till long after dark. Meanwhile take some rest and refreshment, for, believe me, you have something before you."

This advice was so obviously right, that the guide, who was in command of the party, had no hesitation in accepting it.

About six o'clock another start was made. At first, though the weather looked threatening, no serious obstacle presented itself. The snow was somewhat deep on the ground, but there were no serious drifts on their way, a way which, indeed, for some distance from the town lay under the leeward side of a wood. But they had not gone more than a mile and a half when a disastrous change in their circumstances occurred. The wind rose almost suddenly to the height of a gale, and brought with it a fall of snow, separated by the rapid movement of the air into a very fine powder, and working its way through the clothing of the traveller with a penetrating power which nothing could resist. Still, benumbed as they were, almost blinded by the icy particles which were whirled with all the force of the tempest against their faces, they struggled on for more than half the distance which lay between them and their destination. Then the three sailors cried out simultaneously that they must halt, and the guide unwillingly owned that he must follow their example. Only the Saxon was left to go on, and he, with a gesture which it was impossible to mistake, declared his intention of persevering. Just at that moment the clouds parted in the east, and the full moon showed the landscape with a singular clearness, its most conspicuous feature being the gigantic stones of the Great Temple, which could be seen about two miles to the northward. The guide pointed to them, and the Saxon, when they caught his eye, leapt forward with an energy which nothing seemed to have abated, and, with a gesture of farewell to his companions, plunged into the darkness.

CHAPTER XVI.

THE GREAT TEMPLE.

THE Great Temple, or Stonehenge as it is now called, though its decay had already commenced, still preserved the form which we have now some difficulty in tracing.   There was an outer circle consisting of thirty huge triliths,[1] the greater part of which were still standing in the position in which the unsparing labour of a long past generation had placed them.   Within this there was a circle of forty single stones, this circle again containing two ovals. One of these ovals was composed of five triliths, even larger than those which stood in the outer circle ; the other was made of nineteen upright stones.   At the upper end of this stood the altar, a low, flat structure of blue marble.

All the preparations for the sacrifice were complete when Cedric—for we may as well henceforth

---

[1] A trilith consists of two upright stones with a third placed across.

call the Saxon by the name which he bore among his countrymen—reached the spot. Carna was being led by two of the subordinate priests to the altar, where Caradoc stood, robed for the rite which he was about to perform. The sky had now again cleared, and the moon, riding high in the heavens, poured a flood of silver light through the south entrance, and fell on the priest's impassive face as he stood fronting the light, while it glittered on his crown of gold and gave a dazzling brilliancy to his white robe. In his hand he held a knife of flint, with which it was the custom to give the first blow to the victim, though innovation had so far prevailed even in the Druid worship that the sacrifice was completed with a weapon of steel. But this latter lay at his feet, and was concealed by the fall of his robe. It was not, indeed, supposed to be used. The attendants, who were also dressed in white, were rough and brutal creatures, selected for their office because they could be trusted to carry out any orders without remonstrance or hesitation. Yet even they seemed touched by the girl's dignity and courage, as she walked with head erect and unfaltering gait between them. Had she hesitated, or hung back, or struggled, doubtless they would not have hesitated to drag her to the altar; but walking as she did with a proud resignation to her fate, they showed her a rude respect by letting their hands rest as lightly as possible, so as to give no sense of constraint, upon her arms. On either side of the priest stood Martianus and Ambiorix. The younger man had braced himself to what, fanatical patriot as he was, was evidently a hateful task. He looked steadfastly and unflinchingly at the scene; but his face was deadly pale, and the blood trickled down his chin as he bit his lip in the unconscious effort to maintain a stern composure. Martianus was overwhelmed with shame and horror. If there was one softer heart among the "stern, black-bearded kings" who of old in Aulis watched the daughter of Agamemnon die, he must have looked and felt as Martianus did in the Great Temple that night. Cursing again and again in his heart the ambition which had led him to mix himself up with this fanatical crew, but too much a craven at heart to protest, he stood trembling with agitation, mostly keeping his eyes shut or fixed upon the earth, but sometimes compelled by a fascination which he could not resist to lift them, and take in the horror of the scene. Each of the chiefs had an armed attendant standing behind him. Besides these there were no spectators of the scene, though guards were disposed at each of the entrances which led to the central shrine. Even these had been kept in ignorance of what was to be done, and they were too deeply imbued with the traditional awe felt for the Great Temple to think of playing the spy.

THE SACRIFICE.

The priest, after observing the position of the moon, and seeing that the shadows fell now almost straight towards the north, began the invocation which was the preliminary of the sacrifice. It was for this that the Saxon was waiting, as he stood in the shadow of one of the huge triliths. He crept silently out of his concealment, entirely unobserved, so intent were all present on the scene that was being enacted. His first object was the priest. This had been laid down for him in the instructions given him by the peddler before he started; and indeed his own instinct would have dictated the act. The priest put out of the way, the sacrifice would, for the time at least, be stopped; for so high a solemnity could not be performed but by one of the very highest rank. Time would thus be gained, and with time anything might happen. One firm thrust between the shoulders sent the Saxon's sword right through the priest's body, so that the point stood out an inch or two from the priest. Without a cry the man fell forward, deluging with his blood the stone of sacrifice. The ministrants who stood on either side of Carna were paralysed with astonishment and dismay. Before they could recover themselves Cedric had dragged his weapon out of the priest's body, sheathed it, and thrown himself on them. Two blows, delivered almost simultaneously by fists that had almost the force of sledge hammers, levelled them both senseless to

the ground. He then caught the girl up in his arms.
A full-grown woman — and Carna had a stature
beyond the average of her sex—is no light burden,
but Cedric's strength was, as has been said before,
exceptionally great, and now it seemed doubled by
the fierce excitement of the hour. To escape with
her by running was, he knew, impossible. For such
a task no fleetness of foot, no strength, would be
sufficient. To attempt would be to expose himself to
certain death, and Carna to as certain re-capture.
But his quick eye had caught sight of a place where
he might hold out, at least for a time, against a much
superior strength of assailants. One of the triliths
had partially fallen, the huge cross-stone having been
so displaced that it formed an angle with one of its
supports, and so afforded a protection to the back
and sides of a fighter who managed to ensconce
himself in the niche, and who would so have only his
front to protect. Setting Carna behind him, and
making her understand by a movement of the hand
that she must crouch as low as she could upon the
ground, he prepared to hold his position. The odds
against him were not so heavy as might have been
supposed. The two ministrants were unarmed. Of
the four left, the two chiefs and their attendants,
one was a middle-aged man, who had never been
expert in arms ; and who, whatever his skill and
strength, would scarcely have cared to use them in

such a conflict. Ambiorix, indeed, was of another temper. The gloomy, fanatical doggedness with which he had looked on at the preparations for the sacrifice gave way to a fierce delight when he saw an enemy before him with whom he could cross swords. In his inmost soul he had hated the thought of the sacrifice ; but yet the man who had hindered it, and with it the weal of Britain, was a foe whom it would be pleasure to smite to the ground. But fierce as was his temper, it was full of chivalry. He would not dishonour himself by bringing odds against an enemy. Signing to the armed attendants to stand back, he advanced to challenge Cedric. The Saxon, in height and strength, was more than a match for his antagonist. But he was hampered by his position, especially by the presence of the girl. The weapon, too, with which he was armed—a short Roman sword—was strange to him. He thought with regret of his own good steel, an heirloom come down to him from warriors of the past, and inscribed with magic Runic rhymes, that was then lying at the bottom of the Channel. The change, however, was not really so much to his disadvantage as he thought. The stones behind him would have hindered the long sweeping blow which made the great Saxon swords especially formidable. Altogether it might have seemed as if Cedric must inevitably be worsted in the struggle. The British chief, though he hated the customs and even the civilization of the Roman conquerors, had not disdained to learn what they could teach him in the use of arms. They were acknowledged masters in that, and he accepted the maxim that it was right to be instructed even by one's bitterest enemy. Accordingly he knew all that a fencing master could teach him ; and all the Saxon's agility, quickness of eye, and strength, could not counterbalance the advantage. Before many minutes had passed Cedric was bleeding from two wounds, neither of them very serious, but sufficient to hamper and weaken him. One had been inflicted on the sword-arm, and threatened to disable him altogether before long. He felt this himself, and took his resolve. " The curse of Thor upon this foolish toy ! " he cried, in his native tongue, as he threw the short sword straight in the face of his enemy; and followed up the strange missile by leaping on his antagonist, both of whose arms he fastened down to his sides with a supreme exertion of strength. Gigantic strength, indeed, was the only thing which gave so desperate a resort the chance of success, and this might well have failed, if the adversary had not been entirely unprepared for the movement. Once held in this tremendous clasp, Ambiorix was as helpless as a kid in the hug of a bear. Cedric fairly lifted him off his feet, and threw him backwards. His head struck one of the great stones in his fall, and he lay senseless and helpless on the ground.

The struggle was over so quickly that the attendants had no time to interfere; nor when it was finished did they feel any great eagerness to engage so formidable a champion. Still they advanced, and Martianus, who felt himself unable to maintain any longer in the face of what had happened his attitude of inaction, advanced with them. By this time Carna, who had been almost stunned by the rapid succession of startling incidents, had recovered her self-possession. She lifted herself from the ground, and stepped between Cedric and the three antagonists who stood confronting him.

"Martianus," she cried, "what are you doing here? What mixes you up with these horrible doings—you, my father's friend, you, a Christian man?"

The Briton stood silent, cursing in his heart the hideous enterprise which had not even the poor merit of success. He was spared the necessity of speaking by an exclamation from one of the ministrants.

"See!" cried the man, "there is a party coming. It is not likely that they are friends—let us be off."

And indeed the moonlight clearly showed a number of persons who were rapidly advancing up one of the great avenues.

Martianus did not hesitate.

"You are right," he said to the man, "we must

go.   The priest's body must be left.   It is useless to cumber ourselves with the dead; we shall have as much as we can do to escape ourselves, but take the sacred things.   They at least must not fall into the hands of the enemy.   And you," he went on, addressing himself to the two attendants, "take up your master and carry him off.   We have something of a start, and it is possible that they may not pursue us."

His directions were at once obeyed.   The priest's body was stripped of its robes and ornaments. Ambiorix, who still lay unconscious on the ground, was carried by the united efforts of the soldiers and ministrants, and the whole party had started in the direction of Amesbury before the new-comers, who proved to be the priest Flavius, with a party of his people, reached the Temple.

CHAPTER XVII.

THE BRITISH VILLAGE.

THE British priest's home was at a populous village on the banks of the Avon, now known by the name of Netton, and as this was some miles nearer than Sorbiodunum, he determined to take thither the party whom his opportune arrival had rescued from danger. Once arrived there, it would be easy to send a messenger to the town, and await further instructions. A litter was hastily constructed for Carna, who, though her spirits and courage were still unbroken, was somewhat exhausted by excitement and fatigue. The Saxon's wounds were dressed and bound up by the priest, who united some knowledge of medicine and surgery to his other accomplishments, and was indeed scarcely less well qualified for the cure of bodies than of souls. The priest-doctor looked somewhat grave when he saw how deep the sword-cuts were, and how much blood had been lost, but Cedric made light of his injuries, scorned the idea of being carried, and indeed seemed to find no difficulty in keeping close to Carna's litter on the homeward journey.

Netton—we are unable to give the British name of the village—was reached some time before dawn. At sunrise the priest, who had refreshed himself with two or three hours' sleep, was ready to perform his office at his little church. It was the first day of the week, and the building was crowded. It was an oblong building, with a semicircular eastern end, that resembled that kind of chancel which is known by the name of an apse. It had been designed by an Italian builder, who had copied the shape that seems to have been used in the earliest Christian buildings, that of the *schola* or meeting-house of the trade guilds or associations. The body of the building was of timber. The eastern end, or sanctuary, had a little more pretension to ornament; it was of stone, and the walls were hung with somewhat handsome tapestry, wrought with symbolic designs.

Few of the party which had accompanied the priest the night before were prevented by their fatigue from being present. The Britons were always a devout people, and in Netton their priest had gained such an influence over them, that they were exceptionally regular in their religious duties. Carna had been anxious to attend the service, but the priest's wife—he had followed the usual practice of the British Church in marrying before ordination—had absolutely forbidden so unreasonable an exertion. Cedric, who would otherwise have been present in whatever part of the building was open to an unbaptized person, was still buried in a profound slumber. The service was in Latin, a language of which most if not all the worshippers knew enough to be able to follow the prayers. Such portions of the Scriptures as were read were accompanied by the priest with occasional expositions in the British language; and the sermon, except the text, which was in Latin, and taken from the recently published Vulgate of St. Jerome, was wholly in that tongue. The preacher's text was from the Psalms, " Quomodo dicitis animæ meæ, Transmigra in montem sicut passer? " [1] and was mostly concerned with the troubles of the time. He had in an uncommon degree the national gift of eloquence, and stirred the hearts of his hearers to their inmost depths. He warned them that troublous times were approaching, such as neither they nor their fathers had seen were approaching, and that they would have to resist unto blood for the faith into which they had been baptized.

"Antichrist," he cried, adapting to the day, as

---

[1] " How say ye then to my soul that she should flee as a bird unto the hill ? "—PSALM xi. 1.

Christian preachers have done in every age, the language of the apostles—"Antichrist is at hand! You see him in these heathen hosts who are threatening you on every side; these Saxon pirates from the east, who are ravaging our shores; these Pictish ravagers from the north, who every year are penetrating further and further into the land. Yes," he added, with a telling reference to the event of the night before, "and even in apostates of British blood, who have preserved in your midst the hideous superstitions from which our ancestors turned to worship the blessed Christ; and as it was in the days of the blessed Paul, so is it now: 'He that letteth will let till he be taken out of the way.' The Roman power has kept these forces in check, but it will keep them no more. The time is short. They are gathering every day in greater strength, and you must gird yourselves to meet them." Therefore, he went on, they must be strong and quit them like men. They must gird on them, and make complete in every point, their spiritual armour—the helmet of salvation, the sword of the Divine Word, the all-covering shield of faith; nor must they forget the temporal weapons with which the outward enemies who assail the body must be met. "He that hath no sword, let him sell his garment and buy one," cried the preacher, in his final apostrophe to his people, "and he will find that as his day so shall his strength be, and that the Lord can deliver by few as by many, Gideon's three hundred, as by the eight hundred thousand men that drew sword in Israel."

Wrought by the eloquence of the orator to an almost incontrollable excitement, the whole congregation sprang to their feet, as if they were asking to be led at once to the battle. Then, with a sudden change from the stirring tone of the trumpet to the sweet music of the flute, the preacher touched another note. In a pleading voice, almost but never quite broken with tears, he besought them to cleanse their hearts; he reminded them that the armies of the Lamb of God must be clothed in the white robe of righteousness; that purity, tenderness to the weak, charity to the fallen, were as needed for Christ's soldiers as steadfastness and courage, till many a cheek was wet with tears of contrition and repentance.

In the course of the forenoon a fleet-footed messenger was despatched to Sorbiodunum. By the time he reached that town the Count and his party had arrived, excepting one who had been left behind, still too exhausted by his forced march to move. Some, too, had been sent back in the hope that they might not be too late to rescue the stragglers who had perforce been left behind during the journey through the snow. As there was now no immediate necessity of haste, Ælius allowed his followers to rest and refresh them-

selves for the remainder of the day at Sorbiodunum
The following morning he went on to Netton, where he
found, to his great delight, that Carna had apparently
suffered no harm from her perilous adventures. His
gratitude to the Saxon was beyond the power of
words to express. Though it somewhat hurt his
Roman pride that a barbarian should ever have the
strength to hold out when all others fail, he did not
suffer his vexation to take anything from the hearty
warmth of his thanks. Cedric received them with
the courtesy of an equal, a bearing which both
Britons and Italians could not help resenting in their
hearts, while they reluctantly admired his surpassing
strength.

Three days were spent in Netton with much comfort to the party, the priest and his people showing
them as liberal an hospitality as their means admitted, and refusing the recompense which the Count
almost forced upon them,

"Take something for your poor," said Ælius, when
his arguments were exhausted.

"My people," answered the priest, " must not lose
one of the most precious privileges of their Christian
life, the sweet compulsion of having to minister to
the necessities of those who want their help."

" Then you cannot refuse some ornament for your
church," the Count went on.

The good man hesitated for a moment.   His

church was dear to his heart, and he would gladly have seen it made as fair as art and wealth could make it.

" My lord," he replied, after his brief hesitation, "in happier times, and in another place, I would not refuse your generous offer. But now the poorer we are the better. I should like to see our altar-vessels of gold, but it would not be well to tempt the barbarians to a deadly sin, and to expose Christian lives to worse peril than that they now stand in, by such treasures, of which the report could scarcely fail to be spread abroad. Our chalices, and flagons, and patens are now of lead, thinly covered for decency's sake with silver, and they are of no value to any but those who use them. No, my lord, leave our church with at least such safety as poverty can give. But there are places in the world, I would fain believe, though indeed in these days I scarce know where they are, where Christian men worship God in security, and where the treasures of the church are safe from robbery. Let your gift be given there, when you find the occasion. And if you will let me know the place I shall be happy with imagining it, without the anxious care of its custody."

With this answer the Count was compelled to be content, till at least next morning, by which time Carna's ready wit had suggested that the priest could hardly refuse a gift of books.

" My lord," said the good man, when the Count renewed his offer in its fresh shape on the following day, " your determined generosity has overcome me. Books I cannot refuse either for my own sake or my people's. I sometimes feel that they are starved, or at the best ill-fed with spiritual food. I can speak to them of their every-day duties, but I cannot build them up in their faith for lack of knowledge in myself, and where is the knowledge to come from ? Of books I have none but my Bible and my Service-book, and two small books of homilies. If I had some of the commentaries and homilies of the two great doctors of our Church, Hieronymus [1] and Augustine, I should be well content. I have heard of the great preacher of Antioch and Constantinople, John the Golden Mouth,[2] but, alas, I cannot read Greek."

" You shall have them as soon as they can be got," said the Count.

In the course of the day the search party sent back from Sorbiodunum returned. They had found one of the stragglers still alive, and had brought him on to the village where the first halt had been made. There he was being carefully tended, but there was no chance of his being restored to health for many weeks to come. Of the other two they had a terrible

---

[1] Commonly called Jerome.

[2] John Chrysostom, at Antioch 386–398, at Constantinople 398–404.

account to give.   Only a few mangled remains could be discovered, the poor creatures having been manifestly devoured by wolves.   All that could be hoped was that they had expired before they were attacked.

The Count had now nothing to detain him, and as he was for many reasons anxious to be at home, where a multiplicity of duties were awaiting him, he determined to start on the following day.   His route was first to Sorbiodunum.   There he would be on the main road leading to Venta Belgarum.[1]   From Venta, by following another main road he and his party would make their way easily to the Camp of the Great Harbour.

---

[1] Winchester.

CHAPTER XVIII.

THE PICTS.

THE journey to Venta Belgarum was accomplished in safety, and, by dint of starting long before sunrise, in a single day. The distance was a little more than twenty miles, and the road, which was so straight that the end of the journey might almost have been seen from the beginning, lay almost through an open country. This was favourable for speed, as there was little or no need to reconnoitre the ground in advance. It was just after sunrise when the party reached the spot where the traces of the great camp of Constantius Chlorus may still be seen. It had even then ceased to be occupied, but the soldiers' huts were still standing, and the avenues, though overgrown with grass, looked as if they might easily be thronged again with all the busy life of a camp. The Count called a halt for a few minutes, and pointed out the locality to Carna.

" See," said he, with a sigh, "there Constantius had

his camp, the great Constantius to whom we owe so much."

" And was Constantine himself ever there ? " cried the girl, to whom the first Christian Emperor was the object of an admiration which we, knowing as we do more about him, can hardly share.

" I doubt it," returned the Count. " Constantius made it and held it during his campaigns with Allectus. But, my child, I was thinking not of its past, but of its future. It will never be occupied again."

" Why should it ? " exclaimed the girl, almost forgetting in her excitement that she was speaking to a Roman. " Why should it ? Why should not Britain be happy and safe and free without the legions ? Forgive me, father," she added, remembering herself again ; " I am the last person in the world who should be ungrateful to Rome."

" I don't blame you," said the Count, and as he looked at the maiden's flashing eyes and remembered how bravely she had gone through terrors which would have driven most women out of their senses, he thought to himself—" Ah, if there were but a few thousand men who had half the spirit of this woman in them, the end might be different. My child," he went on, " I would not discourage you, but there are dark days before this island. She has enemies by sea and land, and I doubt whether she has the strength to strike a sufficient blow for herself. I am thankful that you will be safely away before it comes."

Carna was about to speak, but checked herself. It was not the time she felt to speak out her heart.

For some time after this little or nothing of interest occurred; but as the party approached within a few miles of Venta the scene underwent a remarkable change. The road had hitherto been almost entirely deserted; it was now thronged : but the face of every passenger was turned towards Venta, not a single traveller was going the other way. Every byway and bridle-path and foot-path that touched the road contributed to swell the throng. In fact, the whole countryside was in motion. And the fugitives, for their manifest hurry and alarm proclaimed to be nothing less, carried all their property with them. Carts laden with rustic furniture, on the top of which women and children were perched, waggons loaded with the harvest of the year, droves of sheep and cattle helped to crowd the road till it was almost impassable. And still the hurrying pace, the fearful anxious glances cast behind showed that it was some terrible danger from which this timid multitude was flying. For some time, so stupified with fear were the fugitives, Ælius could get no rational answer to the questions which he put. "The Picts! The Picts! They are upon us!" at last said a man whom a sudden catastrophe that brought a great pile of household goods to the ground, had compelled to halt, and who was glad to get the help of the Count's attendants to restore them, all help from neighbours being utterly out of the question when all were selfishly intent on saving their own lives and property. When his property had been set in its place again the man thanked the Count very heartily, and was collected enough to tell all he knew.

" There is no doubt that the Picts are not far off. I have not seen anything of them myself, thank heaven! but I could see the fires last night all along the sky to the north."

" Have they ever been here before ? "

"Never quite here. You see, sir, the camp at Calleva [1] kept them in check. A party did slip by, I know, some little way to the westward, and I was glad to hear they got rather roughly handled. But, generally, they did not like to come anywhere near the camps. But now these are deserted, and there is nothing to keep them back."

" But why don't you defend yourselves ? "

" Ah, sir, we have not the strength, nor even the arms. You are a Roman, I see, and, if I may judge, a man in authority, and you know that I am

---

[1] Calleva Attrebatium, now known as Silchester, one of the most perfect specimens of a Roman camp to be seen in this country.

speaking the truth.   You have not allowed us to do anything for ourselves, and how can we do it now at a few months' notice ? "

The Count made no answer ; indeed, none was possible.

" And you expect to find shelter at Venta ? "

" I don't say that I expect it, but it is our only chance.   The place has at least walls."

" And any one to man them ? "

" There should be some old soldiers, but how many I cannot say; anyhow, scarcely enough for a garrison."

When the Count learned the situation he felt that his best course would be to press on with his party to Venta with all the speed possible.   The chief authority of the town was in the hands of a native, who had the title of Head of the City.[1]   It was possible that this officer might be a man of courage and capacity ; but it was far more likely that he would be quite unequal to the emergency.   In either case the Count felt that his advice and personal influence might be of very great use.   Even the twenty stout soldiers whom he had with him would be no inconsiderable addition to the fighting force of the place.   Accordingly he gave orders to his followers to quicken their pace.   Fortunately the greater part

----

[1] Princeps Civitatis.

of the fugitives was behind them ; still it was no easy task for the party to make its way through the struggling masses of human beings and cattle, and it was past sunset when they rode up to the gates of Venta.

It was evident that the bad news had already arrived. The gates were closely shut, while the walls were crowded with spectators anxiously looking northwards for signs of the approaching enemy. The porter was at first unwilling to admit the strangers, peering anxiously through the wicket at them, and declaring that he must first consult his superior. One of the spectators on the wall happened, however, to recognize the Count, and the party was admitted without further question, and rode up at once to the quarters of the Commander of the Town.

If he had hoped to find an official with whom it would be possible or profitable to co-operate in the *Princeps* of Venta, the Count was very much disappointed. He was an elderly man, who had realized a fair fortune by contracting for the provisioning of the army in Southern Britain, and had done very fairly as long as he had nothing to do but execute the orders of the military governor. Left to himself he was absolutely helpless. Indeed he had been taking refuge from his anxieties in the wine-cup, and the Count found him at least half intoxicated. At the moment of the party's arrival the poor creature had reached the valorous stage of drunkenness, and was loud in his declarations that there was no possible danger.

" They will know better," he said, " than to come near Venta. If they do, very few will go back. Indeed I should like nothing better than to give them a lesson. You shall see something worth looking at if you will give us the pleasure of your company in our little town for a day or two."

Another cup, which he drained to the prosperity of Britain and the confusion of her enemies, changed his mood. He now seemed to have forgotten all about the invaders, insisted on recognizing a dear friend of past times in the Count, and invited him to spend the rest of the day in talking over old times.

The Count did not waste many minutes with the old man, but when he left the house the darkness had already closed in. After finding with some difficulty accommodation for Carna, he returned to the gate, anxious to learn for himself how things were going on. He found the place a scene of frightful confusion. The warders had abandoned their office as hopeless. An incessant stream of fugitives, men, women, and children, mingled with carts and waggons of every shape and size, was pouring into the town. Every now and then one of these vehicles, brought out perhaps in the sudden emergency from the repose of years, broke down and blocked the way. Then the living torrent began to rage at the obstacle, as a river in flood roars about a tree which has fallen across its current. Shortly the offending vehicle would be removed by main force, and with a very scanty regard for its contents. Then the uproar lulled again, though there never ceased a babel of voices, cursing, entreating, complaining, quarrelling, through all the gamut of notes, from the deepest base to the shrillest treble. The wall was crowded with the inhabitants of the town, and every eye was fixed intently on the northern horizon. There, as was only too plainly to be seen, the sky was reddened with a dull glow, which might have been described as a sunrise out of place, but that it was brightened now and then for a moment by a shoot of flame. "Where are they?" "How soon will they be here?" were the questions which every one was asking, and which no one attempted to answer. The Count made his way with some difficulty along the top of the rampart in search of some one from whom he might hope to get some rational account of the situation. At last he found among the spectators an old man, whose bearing struck him as having something soldierly about it. A nearer look showed him a military decoration. He lost no time in addressing him.

"Comrade," he said, "I see that you have followed the eagles."

The veteran recognized something of the tone of command in the Count's voice, and made a military salute.

" Yes, sir, so I have, though my sword has been hanging up for more than thirty years."

" And what do you think of the prospect ? "

" Badly, sir, badly. This is just what I feared ; but it has come even sooner than I looked for it. Things have been very bad for some time in the north ever since the garrisons were taken from the Wall,[1] but, except for a troop of robbers now and then, we were fairly safe here. But now that these barbarians know that the legions are gone, there will be no stopping them."

" They are the Picts, I hear. Have you ever had to do with them ? "

" Yes, sir, I have seen as much of them as ever I want to see. I came to this island thirty-nine years ago with Theodosius, grandfather, you know, of the Augustus ; " and the old man, who was steadfastly loyal to the Emperor, bared his head as he spoke. "I am a Batavian from the island of the Rhine, and was then a deputy-centurion in Theodosius' army. We found Britain full of the savages. They had positively over-run the whole country as

---

[1] The wall of Antoninus, built to defend Northern Britain from the Caledonians, and held by Roman forces till far on in the fourth century.

far as the southern sea, and only the walled towns
had escaped them, and these were almost in despair.
I shall never forget how the people at Londinium
crowded about the general, kissing his hands and
feet, when he rode into the town. But I must not tire
you with an old soldier's stories. You ask me about
the Picts. They are the worst savages I ever saw,
and I have had some experience too. They go naked
but for some kind of a skin girdle about their loins,
and they are hideously painted, and their hair is
more like a beast's than a man's, and then they eat
human flesh. Ah, sir, you may shake your head,
but I know it. We used to find dead bodies with
the fleshy parts cut off where they had been. I
shudder to think of what I saw in those days. Well,
we gave them a good lesson, drove them back to their
own country, and an awful country it is, all lakes
and mountains, with not so much as a blade of corn
from one end to the other. But now they will be
as bad as ever."

"But you are safe here in Venta, I suppose ? "

"Safe ! I wish we were. If we had a proper
garrison here, there is no one to command them.
You have seen the *Princeps ?*"

The Count said nothing, but his silence was
significant.

" But there is no garrison. There are not more than
fifty men in the place who have ever carried arms."

" But surely the people will defend themselves. You, as an old soldier, know very well that civilians, who would be quite useless in the field, may do good service behind walls."

" True, sir, if they have two things—a spirit and a leader; and these people, as far as I can tell, have neither."

" That is a bad look out.   But tell me—how soon do you think the enemy will be here ? "

" Not to-night, certainly; perhaps not to-morrow. And indeed it is just possible that they may not come at all.   You see that they get a great quantity of plunder in the country without much trouble or danger, and they may leave the towns alone.   Barbarians mostly don't care to knock their heads against stone walls, and of course they think us a great deal stronger than we are."

After making an appointment with his new acquaintance for a meeting on the following day, the Count rejoined his party.

The next day the *Princeps* called a meeting of the principal burgesses of the town, at which the Count, in consideration of his rank as a Roman official, was invited to attend.   The tone of the meeting was better than he had expected.   There were one or two resolute men among the local magistrates, and these contrived to communicate something of their spirit to the rest.   A general levy of the inhabitants between the ages of sixteen and sixty was to be made. The town was divided into districts, and recruiting officers were appointed for each. By an unanimous vote of the meeting the Count was requested to take the chief command. The delay of the invaders gave some time for carrying out these preparations for defence. A force was speedily raised, sufficient, as far at least as numbers were concerned, to garrison the walls. This was divided into companies, each having two watches, which were to be on duty alternately. The whole extent of work was divided among them, and the town was stored with such missiles as could be collected or manufactured, while Carna busied herself among the women, organizing the supply of food and drink for the guards of the wall, and preparations for the care of the wounded.

CHAPTER XIX.

THE SIEGE.

DAY after day the burgesses of Venta awaited the course of events. For some time they hoped that, after all, the town might not be visited by the invaders. The lurid glow of the skies by night, and the clouds of smoke by day, sometimes borne by the wind so close to the town that the smell could be distinctly recognized, proved that they were still near. But though the effects of their work of ruin were visible enough, of the barbarians themselves no one had yet caught a glimpse. But towards the evening of the seventh day after the Count's arrival a party was seen to emerge from a wood, distant about half a mile from the gates. There were four in all; two of them were mounted on small and very shaggy ponies, the others were on foot. The party advanced till they were about a hundred yards from the wall, and though the fading light prevented them from being seen very clearly, there could be no doubt that they were some of the dreaded Picts.

A debate, which seemed, from the gesticulations of the speakers to be of a somewhat violent kind, was carried on for a time among the savages. Then one of the mounted men rode, with all the speed to which his diminutive horse could be urged, almost up to the gates of the town. He wore a deer-skin robe of the very simplest construction, with holes through which his head and arms were thrust. His legs were bare. Round his neck was hung a bow of a very rude kind. In his right hand he carried a short spear. With the butt of this he struck violently at the gate, as if demanding entrance, and after waiting a few seconds, as it seemed for an answer, turned his pony's head and began to ride back to his party. He had almost reached them before the defenders of the wall had recovered from the astonishment which his audacity had caused them. Then one who was armed with a bow discharged at the retreating figure an arrow, which more by good luck than skill, for scarcely any aim had been taken, struck the Pict on the neck. He did not fall from his horse, but swayed heavily to one side, catching at the animal's mane to steady himself. His three companions rushed forward to help him, and in another moment would have carried him off, but for the resolution and activity of the Saxon, who with the Count was standing on the rampart close to the gate. He lowered himself by his hands from the wall, a height of about fifteen feet, itself no small feat of activity, and ran at his full speed, a speed which, as has been said before, was quite uncommon. Hampered as they were by having to keep their wounded companion in the saddle, the Picts could move but slowly, and were soon overtaken. With two blows, delivered with all his gigantic strength, Cedric levelled two of them to the ground, and, seizing the wounded chief, threw him over his shoulder, then turning ran towards the gate. For a moment the third Pict stood too astonished to move. Cedric had thus a start of some yards, and before he could be overtaken, had got so close to the wall as to be under the protection of the archers and slingers who lined it. The next moment the wicket of the gate was opened, and the prisoner secured.

It was evident that he was a prize of some value, for a rudely wrought chain of gold round his neck showed that he was a chief. He had ridden up to the gate against the advice of his followers, as it was guessed, under the influences of copious draughts of metheglin. The effect of the liquor, together with the pain of his wound and the shock of his capture, had been to make him insensible when he was brought into the town. While he was in this state his wound was dressed by a slave who had some surgical skill, and who declared that though serious it was not mortal. When he recovered consciousness

CEDRIC AND THE PICT.

he behaved more like a wild beast than a man. His first act was to tear furiously at the bandage which had been applied to his wound. The attendants mastered him with difficulty, for he fought with the ferocity of a wild cat, and then bound his hands and feet. Thus rendered helpless, he raved at the top of his voice till sheer exhaustion reduced him to silence, a silence which was soon followed by sleep.

The night passed without any attack. It was evident that the Picts were in considerable force, for their watch fires were to be seen scattered over a wide extent of country, and there was much anxious talk in the town about the chances of a siege. Few indeed in Venta closed their eyes that night, and with the earliest morning the whole town was astir. The invaders, of course, had no notion of how a siege should be conducted, nor had they the necessary mechanical means even if they had known how to use them. Their arrows did but little harm, for their bows were ill made, and had but a small range, nothing like that which was commanded by the better weapons of the defenders. With the sling, however, they were singularly expert, and inflicted no small damage, making indeed some parts of the walls scarcely tenable. But as they could do nothing without showing themselves, they suffered more loss than they inflicted. In the early days of the siege especially, a catapult, which the garrison worked from the walls, did great damage among them. After awhile they were careful not to collect in such numbers as to give a fair mark for this piece of artillery.

The townspeople were greatly elated at their success, and when, about a fortnight after the first appearance of the invaders before the walls, two days had passed without one of them being visible, concluded that, hopeless of making any impression upon the place, they had disappeared.

They were soon undeceived. It was growing dusk on the third day after the supposed departure of the enemy, when a heavily laden cart was drawn up to the western gate of the city. The driver, apparently a country man, knocked for admittance. By rights, at such an hour, it should have been refused, but the vigilance of the watch had begun to slacken, most of the besieged believing that the danger was practically over. Accordingly, no difficulty was made about throwing open the gates. But, once thrown open, they were not so easily closed. Just as the cart was passing through the opening in the wall one of the wheels came off, and the vehicle broke down hopelessly. Commonly it would not have taken long to clear the obstacle out of the way. There was usually a throng of people about the gates and on the walls, and a multitude of willing hands would have been ready to lend their help. But just at this moment the gates and walls were almost deserted. Evensong was going on in the Church of Venta, and a preacher of some local fame was expected to enlarge on the Divine mercy shown in the deliverance of the town from the barbarians. The keepers of the gate would, therefore, have been at a loss even if they had seen the necessity of bestirring themselves. As it was, they were content to do nothing. They amused themselves by standing by and laughing at the rustic driver as he slowly unladed from his vehicle its miscellaneous cargo, the contents, it seemed, of one of the country-side cottages, from which the terror of the invasion had driven their inhabitants. The process of unloading, carried on slowly and with much grumbling, was scarcely half finished, when one of the warders, chancing to look behind him, caught sight of a body of men rapidly approaching through the darkness. A number of Picts had concealed themselves in the wood mentioned before as distant about half a mile from the wall, and when they saw the gate blocked by the broken-down cart— a part, it need hardly be said, of the stratagem—had made a rush to get to it before the obstacle could be removed. A hasty alarm was raised, and some of the citizens who were in hearing ran up. But it was too late. The rustic driver, a villain whose treacherous services had been bought by the enemy, had quickened his work when he saw his employers approaching, and contrived to finish the unloading of the cart at the very moment of their coming up. In a few moments some of them had clambered over the empty vehicle, struck down the guards, and disabled the fastenings of the gates. Before many minutes had passed the whole of the ground outside the gates seemed to swarm with the enemy, and though the townspeople had now begun to make a rally in force, it was too late to make any effectual effort to keep them out. The situation would in any case have been full of danger. At Venta it was hopeless. A garrison of veterans might have kept their heads, but there were not more than sixty or seventy among the defenders of Venta who had ever seen service in the field ; and the citizen soldiers were fairly panic-stricken when they saw themselves actually facing a furious, yelling crowd of barbarians, cruel and savage creatures in reality, and commonly reported to be even worse than they were. Without even striking a blow they turned and fled. The Count, whom the alarm had just reached, was met, and, for a time, carried away by the tide of fugitives. Still he was able to rally a few men to his side for a last effort. Some of his own followers were with him, and the rest could be fetched in a few moments. The gallant old centurion, in spite of his seventy years, was prompt with the offer of his sword ; and, as always happens, the infection of courage spread not less rapidly than the infection of cowardice. Altogether a compact body of about a hundred men were collected. Well armed and well disciplined they turned a steadfast face to the enemy, and were able to make their retreat to a little fort which stood on a hill to the south-east of the town. Carna, the priest of Venta and his family, and a few other non-combatants were with them. More, in the terrible confusion of the scene, it was impossible to rescue. All through the trying time Cedric distinguished himself by his coolness and courage. When once he had seen Carna safely bestowed in the centre of the party, and had also seen that the person of the Pictish chief was secured (having the presence of mind to foresee that he would be a valuable hostage), he took up a position in the extreme rear of the retreat, and performed prodigies of valour in keeping the pursuers at bay.

The occupation of the fort could, of course, do nothing more than give them a breathing space. Though it had been for some time unoccupied, its defences were tolerably perfect, and it might have been held against a barbarian enemy as long as provisions held out. Unfortunately this was the weak part of their position. Of provisions they had very little. Luckily the place had latterly been used as a warehouse, and contained some sacks of flour. A few sheep were feeding in a meadow hard by, and were hastily driven within the defences. Happily there was a well within the walls.

That night was a dismal experience which none of the party ever forgot.   A confused noise came up from the town, where the savages were busy with plunder and massacre.   Every now and then some piercing shriek was heard, curdling the blood of all the listeners.   At other times the loud crash of some falling building could be distinguished.   Towards midnight flames could be seen bursting out from various parts of the town, and before an hour had passed, every eye was fixed on a hideous spectacle, on which it was an agony to look, but from which it yet seemed impossible to turn.   Venta was on fire. The flames could be seen to catch street after street, and distinctly against the lurid background of the burning houses could be seen, flitting here and there, as they busied themselves with the work of destruction, the dark shapes of the barbarians.   When the morning dawned only a few detached buildings, among them the church, a basilica of some size, built by the munificence of the Empress Helena, were standing.

The party in the fort reviewed their position anxiously.   The civilians were for the most part in favour of staying where they were.   They felt the substantial protection of the stout walls which surrounded them, and were indisposed to leave it.   The military men, on the other hand, recognized facts more clearly and more completely.   The protection of the fort was worth this and this only—that it gave them time to reflect. To stand a siege would be to ensure destruction.

"We must cut our way through," said the Count. "If we do not try it now we shall have to try it three or four days hence, and try it with less courage, and hope, and strength, and probably fewer men than we have now."

"Cut our way through all those thousands of savages!" said the *Princeps*, who was one of the few who had escaped from the town. "No; we should be fools to leave the shelter of these walls."

"Shelter!" cried the old centurion; "will they shelter you against famine? No; let us go while we have strength to walk."

"But how," said another of the townspeople, "how will you do all the three things at once—retreat, and fight, and save the women? A few of the men may get through, but it will be as much as they can do to take care of themselves."

The argument was only too clear, and the Count turned away with a groan of despair. The prospect seemed hopeless. All the comfort that he could find was in the thought that he and Carna should anyhow, not fall alive into the hands of the barbarians.

But now Cedric came again to the rescue with the happy thought which had made him carry off the

Pictish chief. He said nothing to any of his companions; but he managed the affair with the prisoner, and managed it with an astonishing speed and success. He pointed to a party of the chief's fellow-countrymen who were approaching the fort, by way, it appeared, of reconnoitring its defences, and intimated that he wished to open communications with them, showing at the same time, by holding up two of his fingers, that not more than two were to approach. The chief, whose intelligence was sharpened by a keen sense of his danger, by a shrill piercing whistle, twice repeated, conveyed this intimation to his countrymen, and two of them approached to within speaking distance of the walls. Cedric now addressed himself to the task of making his prisoner understand that his life and liberty depended upon his inducing his countrymen to retire. This was not very easily done. The expressive gestures of drawing a knife across the throat was readily understood; and at last by a pantomime of signs he was made to comprehend that this would be the result, if his countrymen were to approach the walls. Then the other alternative was expressed. One of the bonds with which he was secured was partially loosed, and this action was accompanied by a sweeping gesture of the hand towards the north, which was to indicate that that must be their way, if he was to be freed. A light of comprehension gradually dawned in the chief's eye, and the Saxon had little doubt that he had made his meaning intelligible. Whether the man could be trusted to keep the engagement was what neither he nor any one could say. But it was clear that the risk had to be run, for the only possible hope of escape lay in this direction. A conversation followed between the chief and his countrymen, accompanied by signs which were intended to convey to the Saxon the purport of what he was saying. When it was over, they disappeared, and the chief, turning to Cedric, raised his hands to the sky in a gesture which the latter interpreted, and rightly interpreted, to mean that he was calling the powers above to witness his fidelity to the engagement which he had made.

Cedric then communicated the result of his negotiations through his interpreter the peddler to the Count. It was not received with unanimous approval by the party in the fort. The *Princeps* especially protested loudly against trusting their lives to the good faith of a couple of savages. "A Pict and a Saxon!" he cried, "the worst enemies that Britain has, and you think that they are going to save us!" He was quickly overruled by the Count, who let him understand quite plainly that he would be left to shift for himself unless he availed himself of this chance of escape.

"Do as you please," was Ælius's first utterance,

"you have authority over the fort, and if you choose to defend it with as many of your friends as you can induce to stay with you, I cannot hinder you. But you must take the consequences, and I haven't the shadow of a doubt what these will be. Meanwhile, I and my party mean to go. As for the Pict, I know nothing of him; the Saxon I would trust with my life, and what is far dearer to me, the life of my daughter. He has proved his good faith already in such a way that I for one shall never doubt him again."

Preparations for departure were hastily made. Indeed there was little to prepare. The party had simply nothing with them except their arms. Every one had to walk—for food they had to trust to what they might find on the road. But before they started the Count loosed with his own hand the chief's bonds. The chief put his hand upon his heart, and then lifted it to the sky with the same gesture of appeal that he made before.

It is sufficient to say that he kept his word, for the party reached the coast without molestation.

CHAPTER XX.

FOR several weeks life passed at the villa with little change or incident. But the Count, though he kept a cheerful face, and talked gaily of the future to his daughter and Carna, felt more acutely every day how full his position was of anxieties and difficulties. First came, as it always does come first, the question of money. It had never been a very easy matter to provide for the expenses of the fleet. Again and again the Count had drawn on his private means, which were happily very large. But these had lately been crippled by the troubled condition of the provinces in which his estates were situated, and even if they had been untouched the burden that now threatened to fall upon them would have been too great for them to bear. Some of the seaport towns would, he hoped, continue to pay their contributions. He was personally popular, and his influence would do something. Then, again, he could still give at least some return for the money. The sea-coast must be protected from the enemy, and no one could protect it so cheaply and so effectually as he. From the inland towns, which had always grumbled at having to pay an impost from which they saw no visible advantage, nothing was to be hoped. And any expectation of money from the authorities at home was quite out of the question.

One thing was quite certain: the establishment must be reduced within much narrower limits. He must diminish the fleet, and lessen also the range of shore which he professed to defend. He could not henceforth pretend to go north of the mouth of the Thamesis. For the coast southward and westward he might be able to provide more or less effectually. More he could not do.

One of the first necessities of the changed position in which he found himself was that he must give up the villa on the east coast. It would be a matter for after consideration whether the island of Vectis was not too much out of the way. But till that point could be settled, it would have to be his head-quarters. To carry out these new arrangements, and to wind up affairs in the region which he was preparing to re-linquish, a voyage became necessary. On this voyage the Count started early in April. He arranged for disposing of that part of the fleet which he could not hope to keep in his own pay. Some of the oldest galleys were broken up; others were handed over to the authorities of the coast-towns, on the understanding that they were to man and pay them themselves. A few picked men were taken from the crews by the Count; the rest, excepting such as were re-engaged by the local authorities, were discharged. When this had been done, and the villa had been dismantled, the Count prepared to return to the island.

Here, meanwhile, there had been trouble. The Saxon had quietly returned to his work at the forge, and would have been perfectly content, as far as could be judged from his demeanour, if only he had been left alone, and permitted to pay as before his distant worship to Carna. But to some members of the villa household he was an object of dislike. They were jealous of the favour in which the Count and the Count's family held him. They were naturally not at all pleased at what they could not but acknowledge his great superiority in strength, and as Christians, though not particularly zealous in their performance of most of their duties, they felt themselves to be unquestionably zealous and sincere in their hatred and contempt for a pagan. The Saxon, on the other hand, heartily despised those by whom he was surrounded. They were slaves, or little better than slaves, and he was a freeman and a chief, though the gods had made him a prisoner.

He went to and fro among them with a scorn which was not the less evident because it was not expressed in words.

For a time this enforced silence helped to keep the peace; Cedric knew nothing of the British tongue, or of the mongrel Latin which sometimes took its place, and the other inhabitants of the villa nothing of Saxon. There were angry and contemptuous looks on both sides, but there was nothing more; or if there were words, these were harmless, because they were not understood. But by degrees this was changed. Cedric had intelligence of no common kind—indeed he was something of a poet among his own people—he had many motives for learning the language of those among whom he dwelt, his adoration for Carna being one of the most powerful, and he had, too, opportunities for learning. The peddler taught him much, and Carna, who never forgot her zealous desire for his conversion, taught him more. The end was that he picked up much of the British language with extraordinary rapidity, and, in little more than six months after his capture, could express himself with some ease and fluency.

This was very well in its way, but it had the unfortunate result that he began to understand and be understood. Every day the relations between him and the domestics and artizans employed about the villa became worse and worse, and it was not long before matters came to a crisis.

Cedric had repeatedly noticed that the tools which he used in the forge had been hidden or mischievously damaged. He was too proud to complain, and indeed his temper was curiously patient in any matter where he did not conceive his honour to be involved. He said nothing about the matter, searched for his missing tools, and if he could not find them, continued to do without them, and repaired the injuries as best he could. The offender, of course, grew bolder with impunity, and at last the limits of Cedric's endurance were reached and passed. Coming into the forge at an unusually early hour one morning, he caught the doer of the mischief in the very commission of a more serious piece of mischief than he had yet ventured, namely, cutting a hole in the bellows. He lifted the offender by the skin of the neck—he was a lad of about sixteen, and son of the chief bailiff of the farm attached to the villa—shook him, as a dog shakes a rat, yet without forgetting that he was but a boy, dipped him head foremost in the bath of the forge, and then let him go, more dead than alive from the fear that he felt at finding himself in the hands of the great giant.

Unluckily at the very moment when the young rascal was being dismissed in a paroxysm of howling with a contemptuous kick, his father entered the yard.   No one about the place was more prejudiced against the Saxon, or more jealous of the favour in which he stood with the Count and his family.   He had too, in its very worst form, the ungovernable Celtic temper, and now, when he saw his son, a spoilt boy whom everybody else disliked, ill-treated as he thought by the prisoner, he was fairly carried out of himself.

"Pagan dog!" he cried, "do you dare to touch with your beast's foot a Christian boy?" and he struck at the Saxon with a long cart whip which he had in his hand.

The end of the lash caught the Saxon's cheek, on which it raised an ugly-looking wheal.   Even in the height of his passion the Briton stood aghast at the change which came in a moment over the form and features of the Saxon.   One or two of the bystanders had seen him face to face with an enemy, and had wondered how strangely calm he had seemed to be, showing no sign of excitement, except a certain glitter in his eyes.   He had a very different look now.   "The form of his visage was changed," as it was in the Babylonian king [1] when he found him-self, for the first time in his life, confronted by a point-blank refusal to obey.   A consuming anger, like the Berseker rage of his kinsmen of after times,

---

[1] Daniel iii. 19.

CEDRIC'S FURY.

the Vikings, seemed to possess and transform him. His features worked, as if caught by some strange malady, his eyes literally blazed with fury, his whole figure seemed to dilate. The luckless bailiff was seized round the middle, lifted from the ground as easily as if he had been a child in arms, and hurled with a crash, like a bolt from a catapult, against the wall. He lay there bleeding from nose and mouth, while the horror-stricken Britons stood helpless and afraid to move.

" Dogs of slaves," cried Cedric, "do you dare to growl at your master; " and he swept through the terrified crowd, laying them low on either side. Happily at the moment he had no weapon in his hand, but he seized a bar of iron from the anvil of the forge, and swinging it round his head, prepared, it seemed, to deal about him an indiscriminate destruction. What would have followed it is impossible to say. In his fury and in his absolute mastery over that shrinking crowd, he was like a tiger in the midst of a flock of sheep. But at the critical moment, before his hand had dealt a single blow, the apparition of Carna interposed between him and his victims. The uproar in the court had reached her in her chamber, and brought her ready to play her accustomed part of peacemaker. Now she stood, her figure framed like a picture, in the door which opened on the court from the part of the villa which she occupied. She wore a simple dress of white, fastened with a blue girdle; her long chestnut hair fell in loose waves to her waist, for she had not had time to arrange it in more orderly fashion. Her face was pale and troubled, her eyes wide open with a sad surprise. It was indeed another Cedric that she saw from the one whom she had known. Was this terrible savage, who looked more like some dreadful spirit from the abyss than a human creature, the gentle giant in whose mute homage she had felt such an innocent pleasure, the hopeful pupil whom she was teaching, as she hoped, to put away savage ways for the mild and peaceful behaviour of a Christian. As for Cedric, he seemed paralyzed at the vision that presented itself to him. The sight of the girl always moved him strangely; now she reminded him of the time when he had first seen her by the bedside of his dying brother; and the remembrance completed, if anything was needed to complete, the impression. The fury that had transfigured him seemed to pass away; his hand loosed its hold on the weapon which he held. His adversaries did not fail to use the opportunity. They had been too genuinely frightened to let it slip when it came. Indeed they may be excused for feeling that this most formidable enemy had to be secured against doing any more damage. The moment they saw him unarmed they sprang with one movement on him and overpowered him.   Even then, if he had offered resistance, they might have had no small trouble, perhaps might have failed in securing him. But he stood passive, and allowed his hands to be bound without a struggle, and followed without difficulty when he was led to the room where offenders were commonly confined. Some of the meaner spirits in the household were disposed to visit their feelings of annoyance and humiliation on his head, now that he seemed to be in their power. But others felt a salutary dread of rousing the sleeping lion whose rage they had seen could be so terrible. Carna too did not abandon her *protegé.* He was chained, indeed, to a staple in the wall of the room which served as his prison. This seemed nothing more than a necessary precaution. But the girl let it be distinctly understood that no cruelty must be used to him, and she took care herself that his supply of food should be plentiful and good.

CHAPTER XXI.

THE ESCAPE.

THE prisoner seemed to submit to his fate with patience. He thanked the attendant who brought him his rations with a nod and smile, and disposed of the food with an appetite which seemed to indicate a cheerful temper. A visit which the peddler paid him the second day of his imprisonment was apparently received as a welcome relief. The two had a long and friendly conversation, nor did Cedric utter a word of complaint against his treatment.

In reality the young chief was keeping under his rage with an effort almost unbearably painful. That he should be chained like a dog to the wall was an intolerable grievance ; he, a free man, and the son of a long line of chiefs which boasted the blood of the great Odin himself ! The iron did indeed enter into his soul, and the seeming calm of his outward patience concealed a whole volcano of inward fury.

It was only the hope of freedom that kept him calm. It was that he might not diminish this hope, this almost desperate chance, by the very smallest fraction that he ate and drank with such seeming cheerfulness. He would want, he knew, all his strength for an escape. He would support it and husband it to the utmost.

And for an escape, unknown to his keepers, he was steadily preparing. The chain which bound him to the wall was fastened round his right arm and leg, and the fastening would have seemed secure to any ordinary observer. But such an observer would not have made the necessary allowance for the young man's ordinary vigour and endurance. His hand was large and muscular; far too much so, one would have thought, to pass through the ring which had been welded round the arms. But he possessed an unusual power of contracting it. To exercise this power was indeed a painful effort, causing something like an agonizing cramp; still it was an effort that could be made, and made without disabling the limb. It could not, however, be done twice, because the hand, recovering its shape from the extraordinary pressure to which it had been subjected, would infallibly swell. Cedric, accordingly, after satisfying himself that it could be done, postponed actually doing it till the moment of escape had arrived. The fastening of the leg was less manageable. He would not have scrupled to do as the Spartan prisoner is said to have done, and cut off the foot which impeded his escape, but he had positively nothing with which this could be done. The only alternative was to drag the staple from the wall, and to carry it and the chain along with him. Fortunately, strong as it was, it was light. The staple at first seemed obstinate. It had indeed been subjected to tests which satisfied the villa blacksmith of its capacity of resistance. But repeated efforts, made with all the enormous strength which the young giant could bring to bear, weakened its hold, and at last it gave. The prisoner was prudent enough not to complete the separation of the iron from the walls. It would have been difficult to replace it so as to escape the notice of the attendant. Accordingly the drag was relaxed as soon as the first indications of yielding were felt. The time for attempting the escape was a subject of much anxious deliberation. The obvious course would have been to choose some hour between midnight and dawn; but Cedric had heard from time to time the step of some one walking up and down before his prison, and he guessed that it might be guarded at night, but left during the day-time, on the presumption that the captive would scarcely make an effort to escape while it was light. It was this accordingly that he resolved to do. Shortly after sunrise the attendant paid him his customary visit, bringing with him the morning meal. Cedric pretended to be but half awake, and, returning his salutation in a mumbling, sleepy tone, turned again on his side, as if to continue his slumbers. But the moment after the man had left the room he was at work. He dragged his hand through the ring, at the cost of a pang which taxed his endurance to the utmost; pulled the staple from the wall, wound the chain round his leg, and wrenching away one of the iron bars of the window, dropped through the opening thus made on to the ground. His calculation was correct. The ground was clear. Then another question presented itself to him. Should he attempt to escape as he was? He knew where a boat was commonly kept, and it had been his plan to take this and row out to sea in the hope of meeting some one of his countrymen's galleys. If he once got off from the shore he was free, for if the worst came to the worst, he could at least die as a free man should. But should he go unarmed, and with the hampering chain about his leg? A moment's consideration—no more was possible—decided him. He would make one more bold effort. The forge was close at hand, and he knew from having worked there that at that hour in the morning it was commonly empty, the workmen leaving it for their morning meal. There he could find what he wanted, a file to release himself from the chain, and a weapon.

The forge was empty, as he had expected. The question was, How long would it remain so? The workmen, he could see, had but just left it. The fire had not died down to the lowest, showing that the bellows had been recently at work, and a piece of iron that had been left, half-wrought, on the anvil, was still hot, as he could feel from putting his hand near it. It might be safest to take a file and escape with it at once. On the other hand, it would be far better to release himself at once from his encumbrance, in the event of having to run or fight for his life. He might count, he thought, upon half an hour, and he resolved to file away the chain then and there. With admirable coolness he sat down and applied all the strength and skill which he possessed to the work, and had finished it in little more than half the time which he had reckoned to have undisturbed. He then caught up a sword which hung on one of the walls. It was an old-fashioned weapon, but Cedric, who knew good iron when it came in his way, had tried its temper, and knew it to be capable of doing good service.

So far everything had favoured him, nor did his good fortune desert him now. He found the boat, which was one commonly used for fishing by the inmates of the villa, ready furnished with oars and a small mast and sail. There were even, by good luck, a small jar of water, some broken food in a hamper, left by a party which had been using it the day before, with some fishing lines. These, Cedric thought to himself, might be useful if he failed to fall in with any of his countrymen.

Jumping on board, he plied his sculls rapidly, going in the direction of the sea, and keeping as close under the shore as possible, so as to be out of sight of the villa. As it happened, this precaution was unnecessary. His absence was not discovered till shortly after noon, when the attendant, bringing the midday meal, was astonished beyond measure to find the room empty. But another danger threatened him, a danger which he had not indeed forgotten, but against which he had known it to be impossible to take any precautions. This was the chance of meeting with the Count's squadron as it was returning to the island ; and it was this that he actually encountered.

Just as he had reached the mouth of the Haven and was turning his boat eastward, he saw within a hundred yards of him one of the Roman galleys. It was not the Count's own vessel, for this had been delayed by an accident to the rigging, and was now many miles behind, but was in charge of the second-in-command. The recognition was mutual. Cedric's tall figure was not one that could be easily mistaken, nor could it be doubted that he was attempting an escape. Had the Count been there he would probably have parleyed with the fugitive. The officer in command was not so considerate.

"Shoot," he cried, "he is trying to escape," and as he spoke he seized a bow which lay on deck, and took aim at the Saxon. His order was immediately observed, and a shower of missiles was directed at the boat. They all fell short, for Cedric had by this time increased his distance. In a minute or two, however, the ship was put about, and then began to gain rapidly on the solitary rower.

Another volley was discharged, and this time one of the arrows took effect, wounding the fugitive slightly in the left arm. The situation was desperate. To remain in the boat was to await certain death. A third volley would unquestionably be fatal. Cedric jumped overboard, but still clung to the side of the boat. It was only just in time. The third volley was discharged, and rattled on the upturned keel of the boat so thick as to show plainly what the fate of the occupant would have been. Still, though he had escaped for the moment, Cedric's fate seemed sealed. The boat had given him shelter for the time, but to go on clinging to it would be to ensure his capture. He left it, and after making a few vigorous strokes, threw up his arms from the surface of the water, and uttering a loud cry, disappeared.

His quick eye had discerned a great mass of sea-weed floating on the water. about fifty yards away,

Cedric's Escape.

and his ready intelligence had seen a chance, small indeed and almost desperate, but still a chance of escape. Swimming under water to the sea-weed, he was able to come to the surface and to take breath under its shelter.

On board the galley every one of course supposed him to have sunk. His action of the lifted arms and the loud cry had been natural enough to deceive the most wary observer. The boat was righted and secured by a rope, and the galley pursued its way to the villa, while Cedric was left to make the best of his way to the land.

CHAPTER XXII.

A VISITOR.

THE day after Cedric's disappearance the Count returned to the island. The prospect before him had not by any means lightened. Britain, conquered, oppressed, protected, for nearly four hundred years, governed sometimes ill and sometimes well, according to the varying characters of the Roman legates, but never allowed to do anything for herself, was not ready at a moment's notice to be independent and stand alone. The Count was much too shrewd a man to hope that she would. Still, even he had not realized how bad things would be; and when he came to see them face to face he felt something like disappointment, and even despair. A man will often make up his mind to the general fact of failure, and yet be almost as much vexed at the details of failure, when it comes, as if he had expected success.

The fact was that the Count had found little or no disposition in the native States to take up and carry on the work which he was being compelled to give up. They would make no sacrifices, or even efforts. They refused to work together. Each reckoned on its own chance of escaping the common danger, and would not contribute to the defence that might possibly be wanted for its neighbours, and not for itself. Then jealousies and enmities, hitherto kept in check by the strong hand of a master, began to break out. The cities seemed likely, not only not to combine against Picts and Saxons, but actually to go to war among themselves. The Count felt all the pain that comes to an honest and capable man when he has to face the breaking up of a bad system which he has inherited from predecessors less high principled than himself. It happens very often that revolutions come in the days, not of the worst offenders, but of the men who are making sincere endeavours to do their duty. And so it was with the Count.

It was in a very gloomy and depressed condition of mind, therefore, that he returned to the villa. And almost every day brought news of fresh troubles and disasters. Some of the Roman houses scattered through the country had been attacked and burnt of late. Since the central authority had been weakened the Roman residents had sometimes begun to behave in a lawless and oppressive way to their British neighbours, and these were taking their revenge with the cruelty that is always natural to the oppressed.

Tragical tales of villas surrounded by infuriated crowds of Britons, of masters and families shut up within the walls, and perishing in the fires that consumed them, were brought to the Count by the scared survivors who had contrived to escape from the general destruction.

The Count's personal difficulties were considerable. He had a considerable colony now settled near the villa, and many of its members were helpless and dependent people. The question of feeding them would soon become an urgent one. At present he could use the surplus stores which would no longer be wanted now that his squadron had been so reduced in strength. And there was another question that pressed upon his mind—that of defence. Already he had had to contract his operations. With single pirate vessels, or even small squadrons of two or three, he would be able to deal, but anything stronger would have to be left alone. With the few ships that were left to him it would be madness to run any risk. And what, he could not help thinking, if the Saxons were to attack the villa itself? It had been built as a pleasure residence, and though now fortified as far as circumstances permitted, could not be held against a strong force. Should he continue to occupy, or should he retire to the camp of the Great Harbour, which would at least be a more defensible position?

It may easily be imagined that these anxieties, which had been troubling his thoughts during the whole time of his absence, were not relieved when he heard the story of what had happened during his absence. He owed the Saxon more than he could ever repay, for he shuddered to think what would have happened to Carna but for his strength and energy. And apart from this feeling of gratitude, he admired the man's splendid courage and tenacity. He had even come to rely upon him for services of unusual difficulty and danger. And now, to think that he was lost to them by the stupid perversity and jealousy of a set of slaves!

The said slaves had a bad time with their master for some days after his return. Good-humoured and kind as he was, yet he was a Roman—in other words, he had inherited the lordly temper of a race which had ruled the world for five hundred years, and any contradiction that thwarted him in one of his serious convictions or purposes, broke through the veneer of refinement and culture that commonly concealed the sterner part of his nature. A Christian master could not crucify an offender—indeed, cruci-fixion had been long since forbidden by the law—but he had almost unlimited power over life and limb. Life, indeed, the Count was too conscientious a follower of his religion to touch, but he had no scruple about going to the very utmost verge of severity in the use of minor punishments. As for his daughter, she was only too like her father to be any check on his anger, and for the first time in her life Carna found her mediation useless.

"Girl," he said to her on one occasion, when she had urged her intercession with tears, "you do not know what mischief these foolish, cowardly knaves have done. One thing I see plainly, that as soon as ever the Saxons know the weakness of the position we shall not be able to hold it any longer. There is nothing to hinder them from coming and burning the whole place over our heads; nothing in the way of fortifications, and certainly nothing in the way of garrison. They did not know all this before, but they are sure to know it soon; and we shall see the consequences before many months are over."

In the course of the summer occurred an incident which diverted the Count's attention for a time, though it did not lessen his perplexities.

One morning a small trading vessel entered the haven near the villa. Her business, it was found, was to land a stranger, who had bargained for a passage to the island. The trader had come from a port of Western Gaul, and had then taken her passenger on board. Who he was the captain could not say, except that he had the appearance of a Roman gentleman. The day after they had set sail an illness, which had evidently been upon him when

he came on board, had increased to such an extent
that he had lost consciousness. Two or three days
of delirium had been succeeded by stupor; in this
condition the unfortunate man still lay. But while
still conscious he had written down his destination,
and added an appeal to the compassion of his future
host. The Count read on the paper which the
merchant captain handed to him a few words written
in a trembling hand. They ran as follows :—

*" In case I should not be able to speak for myself, I
invoke by these words the compassionate protection of the
Count Ælius. Let him not fear to receive me, but believe
that I am unfortunate rather than guilty, and that there
is between us the tie of a great common affection."*

The Count did not recognize the stranger, though
a dim impression of having seen him before floated
across his mind; and there was something in his
appearance which agreed with the trading captain's
conviction that he was a man of birth and position.
In any case Ælius was not one who was inclined to
resist such an appeal to his compassion. The
stranger, still unconscious, was landed, together with
a few effects which were said to belong to him, and
at once handed over to the care of Carna. All her
diligence and watchfulness as a nurse, and all the
skill of the old physician, were wanted before the
patient could be brought back to life. For fourteen

days he lay hovering on the very verge of death, mostly sunk in a stupor so complete that it was barely possible to perceive either pulse or breath; sometimes muttering in delirium a few broken sentences, of which all that physician and nurse were able to distinguish was that they were certainly Latin, and that they seemed to be verse.

It was on the morning of the fifteenth day that there came a change. Carna sat by the window of the sick man's room. It had a southern aspect, and the sunshine came with a softened brilliance through the thick tinted glass, and brought out the exquisite tints of the girl's glossy hair, as she sat bending over the embroidery with which she was employing her nimble, never-idle fingers.

" By heaven ! another, fairer Proserpine ! " said the sick man.

The girl turned her head at the sound of the clearly pronounced words which her practised ear distinguished at once from the strained or blurred utterances of delirium.

She held up her finger to her lips. "Do not speak," she said; " you have been very ill, and must not tire yourself."

" Lady," said the sick man, with a smile, " you must at least let me ask you where I am."

" Yes, you shall hear, if you will promise to ask no more questions, but to be content with what you are told. You are with friends, in the island of Vectis, in the house of Ælius, Count of the Saxon Shore. And now be quiet, and don't spoil all our pains in making yourself ill again."

She gave him a little broth which was being kept hot by the fire in readiness for the time when he should recover consciousness; and after this had been disposed of, and she had found by feeling his pulse that he was free from fever, a small quantity of well diluted wine.

"And now," she said, "you must sleep"—a command which he was ready enough to obey.

After this his recovery was rapid. For a time, indeed, the cautious old physician, though he did not forbid conversation, prohibited any reference to business. "You will want, of course," he said, "to tell your story, and to make your plans for the future; that will excite you, and, till you are stronger, may bring about a relapse. Be content for a while with the ladies' company"—Ælia, now that no nursing had to be done, was often with her foster-sister—"the Count will see you when I give permission."

And much talk the ladies had with him, and greatly astonished they were at the variety and brilliance of his conversation. He seemed equally familiar with books and men. He had read everything—so at least thought the two girls, who were sufficiently well educated to recognize a full mind when they came across it—he had been everywhere, he had seen everybody. He never boasted of his intimacy with great people, and indeed very seldom mentioned a name, but his allusions showed that he was equally familiar with courts and camps. It would have puzzled more experienced persons than the sisters to guess who this man of the world, who was also a man of letters, could possibly be.

At the end of another week the physician removed his prohibition, and the Count, who had hitherto judged it better not to agitate his guest by his presence, now paid a visit to his room.

After a few kindly inquiries as to his health, the Count went on, " Understand me, sir, that I have no wish to force any confidence from you. My good fortune gave me the chance of serving you, but it has not given me the right of asking you questions which you might not care to answer. You are welcome to my hospitality as long as you choose to remain here, and you may command my help when you wish to go. But of course, if you care to give me your confidence, it may make the help a great deal more effective."

"Yours is a true hospitality," answered the stranger, with a smile, " but it is right that you should know who I am, and how I came to be here; and I have only been waiting for the good Strabo's leave to tell you. But may your daughter and her sister be present? I have a sad story to relate, but there is nothing in it which is unfit for them to hear, and they have been good enough to show some interest in an unhappy man.

"They shall come, if you wish it," said the Count, "indeed they have been almost dying of curiosity."

It was to this audience that the stranger told his story.

CHAPTER XXIII.

THE STRANGER'S STORY.

" I HAVE found out that my name is known to these ladies, though they are not aware that it belongs to me. You, sir, have very probably not found time among your many cares to give any thought to the trifles which, if I may say so much of myself, have made me famous. I am Claudius Claudianus."

" What! the poet!" cried the Count, "the Virgil of these later days ? "

The poet blushed with pleasure to hear the compliment, which, extravagant as it may seem to us, did not strike him as being anything out of the way. For had not his statue been set up in Trajan's Forum at Rome, an honour which none of his predecessors had been thought worthy to receive ?

" Ah! sir," he replied, "you are too good. But it would have been well for me if I had contented myself with following Virgil ; unfortunately I must also imitate Juvenal. Praise of the fallen may be for-

given, but there is no pardon for satire against those that succeed. Enmity lasts longer than friendship, and I have made enemies whom nothing can appease."

"But what of Stilicho?" said the Count. "Surely he has not ceased to be your friend. Doubtless you owe much to him, but he owes more, I venture to say, to you. He may have given you wealth, but you have given him immortality."[1]

---

[1] It may be as well to say a few words about Stilicho. He was the son of a Vandal captain, and attracted by his skill and courage the favourable notice of the Emperor Theodosius, who gave him his niece Serena in marriage. His influence continued to increase, and in course of time Theodosius made him and his wife guardians of his young son Honorius, whom he shortly afterwards proclaimed Augustus, and Emperor of the West. In 394 Theodosius died, and the Empire was divided between his two sons, Honorius taking the West and Arcadius the East. Stilicho's daughter Maria was now betrothed to Honorius, and his influence continued to increase. He restored peace to the Empire, conquering the Franks, chastising the Saxon pirates, and driving back, it is said, the Picts and Scots from Britain by the very terror of his name. For six years (398-404) he was engaged in a struggle with Alaric, King of the Goths, over whom he won, in the year 403, a great victory at Pollentia, near the modern Turin, and whom he defeated again in the following year under the walls of Verona. He is said to have conceived the idea of securing the Empire for his own son, and for this purpose to have entered into intrigues with his old enemy Alaric. However this may be, it is certain that he fell into disgrace. His end is related in this chapter. The poet Claudian employed himself in writing the praises of Stilicho and invectives against his rivals Rufinus and Eutropius.

"Ah! sir," said Claudian, "have you not then heard?"

"Heard!" cried the Count; "we hear nothing here. We always were cut off from the rest of the world; but for the last nine months we might as well have been living in the moon, for all that has reached us of what is going on elsewhere."

"You did not know, then, that Stilicho was dead?"

"Dead! But how?"

"Killed by the order of the Emperor."

"What! killed? by the Emperor's orders? It is impossible. The man who saved the Empire, the very best soldier we have had since Cæsar! And you say that the Emperor ordered him to be killed?"

The Count rose from his seat, and walked about in incontrollable emotion.

"So they have killed him! Fools and madmen that they are! There never was such a man. I knew him well. He was always ready, always cheerful, as gay in a battle as at a wedding; as brave as a lion, and yet never doing anything by force that he could contrive by stratagem. But tell me—they had, or pretended to have, some cause. What was it?"

"They said he was a traitor, that he wanted the Empire for himself, or for his son, that he intrigued with the barbarians."

"Well, he was fond of power; and who can wonder

that he was dissatisfied when he saw in **what** hands it was lodged ?   But tell me—what do you think ? "

" I don't say," resumed Claudian, "that he was blameless, but he had an impossible task—he had to save the Empire without soldiers. He did it again and again ; he played off one barbarian power against another with consummate skill; and filled his legion one day with the enemies whom he had routed the day before. But this could not be done without intrigues, without devices which, taken by themselves, looked like treason. But it is idle to speak of the past. He lies in a dishonoured grave, and the Empire of Augustus is tottering to its fall."

" Tell me of his end," said the Count. " You saw it ? "

" Yes," said the poet ; " I saw it, and, I am ashamed to say, survived it. Well, I will tell you my tale. You know he might have had the Empire ; the soldiers offered it to him ; Alaric and his Goths would have been delighted to help him. But he refused. He was loyal to the last. He would not even fly. There are many places where he would have been safe——"

" Yes," interrupted the Count ; " he would have been safe here, if I know anything of Britain."

" Well, he would go to none of them. He went to the one place where safety was impossible. He went to Ravenna ; and at Ravenna every one, from the Emperor down to the meanest slave, was an enemy. He wanted to make them trust him by trusting them—as if one disarmed a tiger by going into his lair! He had two or three of his chief officers with him, besides myself, and as many slaves. We had not a weapon of any kind among us. Stilicho made a point of our being unarmed. Well, we had not an encouraging greeting when we entered the city. Every one, as you may suppose, recognized him. Indeed, there was no man, I suppose, in the whole Empire, who was better known. No one who had ever seen Stilicho could forget that towering form, that white head.[1] There were sullen looks as we walked through the streets, and hisses, and even some stone throwing. However, we got safe to our lodgings, and passed the night without disturbance. The next day, as we were standing in the market-place, an old Vandal soldier—one of the general's countrymen, you know—put a flower in his hand as he walked by, without saying a word, or even looking at him; for it would have been as much

---

[1] " Stilichonis apex et cognita fulsit
Canities."

" There shone Stilicho's towering head and well-known locks of white " — a passage quoted from Claudian by D'Israeli, with exquisite propriety, in his eulogium on the Duke of Wellington, in the House of Commons, November, 1852.

as his life was worth to be seen communicating with us. ' An old comrade,' said Stilicho, who never forgot a face. ' He served with me in Greece.' The flower was a little red thing; the ' shepherd's hour-glass' they call it, because it shuts when there is rain coming. It was a warning. There was danger close at hand. The general said, ' We must take sanctuary.' Then he called me to him. ' Leave me, Claudian,' he said; ' you cannot take sanctuary with us, for you are not a baptized man. I do not count much on the Church's protection; but still it may give me time to make my defence to the Emperor. So you must look out for your own safety. But surely they can't be base enough to harm you, for what you have done?' ' I don't know about that, my Lord,' I answered; ' you remember the fable of the trumpeter.[1] Anyhow, I shall follow you as far as I can.' Well, he went into the great church—what used to be the Basilica before Constantine's time— and took sanctuary by the altar. I did not go further than the nave. In the course of an hour or so comes the bishop, with the archdeacon and two or three priests, and following them one of the great officers of the Court, with a body-guard. The church was

---

[1] In one of Æsop's fables, a trumpeter, taken prisoner, begs for his life, pleading that he has never struck a blow in battle; but is told that he has done much worse in encouraging others to fight by his martial music.

now crowded from end to end ; the people had climbed up into the pulpit, and every accessible spot from which they could get a view of what was going on. I think that there was a reaction in the general's favour. No one, whose heart was not flint, could see the man who had saved the Empire, and that not once or twice, a suppliant for his life. Well, I could not see for myself what went on, but I heard the story afterwards. The bishop brought a safe - conduct from the Emperor ; or rather the chamberlain brought it, and the bishop gave it to Stilicho, with his own guarantee. I can't believe that a man of peace and truth, as he calls himself, could have been a party to so base a fraud—he must have been deceived himself. Well, the safe-conduct promised that the general should be heard in his own defence ; and he wanted nothing more. I doubt whether a trial would have served him ; but they never intended to give him even so much. As soon as he was out of the church I could see what was meant, for I followed him. The chamberlain's body-guard drew their swords. Well, I was wrong to say that he had no friends in Ravenna. He had a friend even in that crew of hirelings—another of his old soldiers, I daresay. I told you that Stilicho had neither armour nor weapon. Well, in a moment, no one could see how, there was a long sword lying at his feet. He took it up ; and, verily, if he had used it, he would at least have sold his life dearly. The general was a great swordsman, as good a swordsman as he was a general. But no; he would not condescend to it ; after a soldier's first impulse to take the weapon, he made no use of it. He pointed it to the ground, and stood facing his enemies. Ah ! it was a noble sight—that grand old man looking steadfastly at that crew of murderers. For a few moments they seemed cowed. No one lifted his hand—then some double-dyed villain crept behind and stabbed him. He staggered forward, and immediately there were a dozen swords hacking at him. At least his was no lingering death. They cut off that grand white head and carried it to the Emperor; his body they threw into the pit where they bury the slaves. And that was the end of the saviour of the Empire."

"And about yourself ? " said the Count.

" Well," went on the poet, " I have since thought that if I had been a man I should have died with him. But when I knew that he was dead, I was coward enough to fly. You would not care to hear how I spent the next few days. I had a few gold pieces in my pocket, and I found a wretched lodging in one of the worst parts of the city, and I lay there in hiding. One day I was having my morning meal at a wine shop, when a shabbily dressed old man, who sat next, turned to me in a meaning way, and, pouring a few drops out of his wine cup, said, ‘To Apollo and the Muses.’   That is a crime now-a-days, in some places at least, Ravenna among them; and he wanted, I suppose, to put me at my ease.   ‘Will you not do the same,’ he went on, ‘of all men in the world there is no one who has better cause.’   Pardon me, illustrious Count, if I repeat his flatteries.   ‘Whom do you take me for?’ said I, for one gets to be a sad coward after a few days’ hiding, and I was unwilling to declare myself.   He replied by repeating some of my verses in so meaning a way that I could not misunderstand him.   ‘These wine-bibbers here,’ he went on, ‘don’t know one verse from another, but they might catch up a name.   Come along with me; I will give you a flask of something better than this sour stuff.’   Well, we went to his house, which was close to the harbour.   He was the owner, I found, of two or three small trading vessels.   The house was a veritable temple of the Muses, ornamented with busts of the poets—my own I was flattered to see among them —and containing an excellent library of books. Manlius—that was my friend’s name—had heard me recite at Rome; and he recognized me partly from memory, partly from my resemblance to the bust. To make a long story short, he entertained me most hospitably for several days, while we discussed the question what was to become of me.   Home I could not go, not, at least, till there should be a change in the Emperor's surroundings. The further I got from Italy the more chance there would be of safety. We thought of North-western Gaul or Britain, or of getting across the Rhine. The end of it was that the good fellow took me across Italy, disguised as his servant, to Genoa, where he had correspondents. From Genoa I went to Marseilles, and from Marseilles overland to Narbonne, using now the character of a bookseller's agent, one which I thought myself better qualified to sustain than any other. At Narbonne I found employment as a bookseller's assistant, till I could get a letter from my wife in Africa with some money. That came in due course, and then I set off on my travels again, still working northwards. Then, sir, I thought of you. I had often heard the great man speak of you. You served under him against the Bastarnæ,[1] I think, and it occurred to me that for Stilicho's sake you might give me shelter. Not that it matters much to me. To Stilicho I owe so much that I can scarcely imagine life without him. He gave me honour, wealth, even," added the poet, with a sad little smile, " even my wife, for it was not my courting, but the Lady Serena's[2] letter that won her for me. But to go on,

---

[1] A tribe that occupied a region included in what is now known as Russian Poland.

[2] Serena was wife to Stilicho, and, as has been said before, niece to the Emperor Theodosius.

I found an honest trader, and bargained with him to bring me here. I had been sickening for some time, and I remember little or nothing from the time of my embarking. There, sir, you have my history carried up to the latest point."

" We will put off the future to another day," said the Count ; " meanwhile you may count on me for anything that I can do."

" Your kindness does much to reconcile me to life," said the poet, " and now I will retire, for I feel a little tired."

" Ah," said Carna half to herself, when he had left the room, " now I understand about Proserpine."

" About Proserpine? What do you mean ? " asked Ælia.

" Why, when he came to himself for the first time I was sitting in the window with a piece of embroidery work in my hand, and I heard him whisper something about Proserpine." Carna suppressed the flattering epithet. " Don't you remember that passage where he describes the tapestry which Proserpine was working for her mother, and how we admired it, and thought we would work something of the kind for ourselves, only we could not get any design ? "

" Yes, I remember," replied the other, " and you have had a Pluto, too, to carry you off. Luckily he was not so successful as the god."

CHAPTER XXIV.

THE Count's difficulties did not seem to diminish as the year advanced. Money grew scarcer and scarcer, till it was only by pledging his personal credit to the merchants of Londinium and other towns in Britain that he was able to find the pay for the crews of his little squadron. His credit happily was still good, a character of twenty years without a single suspicion on his integrity standing him in good stead. Then a disaster happened to one of the few ships that he had retained. After a fierce encounter with a Saxon galley, in which its crew had been much weakened, it had been caught in a storm and driven on the deadly western shore of the island, still dreaded under the name of the Needles by those who navigate the Channel. The ship became a complete wreck and only a small portion of the crew escaped with their lives, all the disabled men being lost.

But the Count's chief perplexities were within

rather than without. For more than twenty years
he had yielded an unquestioning obedience to the
authorities at home. It is true that very little had
been demanded of him. He had been given a free
hand, and left to do his duty with very little interference, if with very little help. But now in the news
of Stilicho's death his loyalty had received a tremendous shock. How was he to bear himself to a ruler
who was capable of committing so great a crime?
True, he knew enough of the Emperor to be sure
that he was only a tool in the hands of others, but
this did not make the matter one whit better. Such
tools are often more mischievous than men who are
actively wicked. What then was he to do? Should
he join the usurper Constantine, of whose astonishing
success in Gaul and Spain he had heard the most
glowing reports? His pride forbad it—an Ælius
doing homage to a man who but twelve months
before had been a private soldier! The thought was
impossible. Should he retire into private life? But
would not that be to shirk his duty, not to mention
the fact that to retire is the one thing which in
troubled times a man in a conspicuous position cannot do. One thing, indeed, was evident—that a
decision would have to be made speedily. His position was rapidly becoming untenable, and he would
have to make up his mind, without much delay,
as to the best way of getting out of it. In the end

it happened to him as it happens to so many of us, that his mind was made up for him.

One day, towards the end of August, he was about to seek in a day's sport a little relief from his many cares. It was still about four hours to noon, and he was sitting under a cherry tree (one of his own planting) in the villa garden, and sharing a slight meal of milk and wheaten cakes with his daughter and Carna, both of whom he had persuaded to accompany him. A young Briton stood by holding in a leash a couple of dogs very much like the greyhounds of our own times; another carried a bow and a quiver; a third had a game bag of leather, with a netted front, slung across his shoulders.

The sailing-master of one of the galleys approached and saluted.

"There is a galley," he said, "coming up the Haven, and I thought that you should know at once, since it seems to have something of importance on board."

"What makes you think so?" said the Count.

"I have been watching it for the last hour," said the man. "At first I thought it was a little trading vessel; but I noticed that as soon as it entered the Haven it hoisted the Labarum."[1]

"The Labarum!" exclaimed the Count; "I have

---

[1] The Imperial standard (see page 21).

not seen that flying from any mast but my own for a year past. Well, that ought to mean something."

It was the etiquette to go as far as was possible to meet an Imperial messenger, just as a host receives a very distinguished guest on his door-step, and the Count, after hastily exchanging his hunting-dress for a toga, went to the little pier at which the galley would land its passenger. He had not to wait many minutes before it arrived, and a handsome young man, with a short military cloak over his traveller's dress, leapt lightly ashore. The Count saluted. The stranger, who was for a time the representative of the Emperor, received the greeting with the dignified gesture of a superior.

"Do I address Lucius Ælius, Count of the Saxon Shore?" he asked.

"I am he," the Count briefly replied.

"I bring the commands of Augustus," said the messenger, producing from a pocket in his tunic a vellum roll, bound with a broad purple cord, and bearing the Imperial seal.

The Count received the missive with a profound inclination, and put it to his lips. At the same time the messenger uncovered, and changed his haughty demeanour for the behaviour usual to a young officer in the presence of his superior.

"It will be more respectful and more convenient to read his Majesty's gracious communication in private. Will you please come with me to my house ? "

He led the way to the villa, and introduced the visitor into the little room which he used for the transaction of business. He then cut with his dagger the purple cord which fastened the package containing the despatch, and, after again putting the document to his lips, proceeded to read it. Its contents were seemingly not agreeable, for his face darkened as he went on. He made no remark, however, beyond simply asking the messenger—

" May I presume that you have a general acquaintance with the contents of this document ? "

" I have," replied the young man.

" Then you will know that the answer is not one which can be given in a moment. But," and he went on with a rapid change of voice and manner, "*cras seria.*[1] I was just on the point of going out for a few hours' hunting when your arrival was announced. Will you come with me ? I have nothing very great to show you, though we have some big game here too, if we had time to look for it, but if you will condescend to anything so small as hare-hunting, I can show you some sport."

The Imperial messenger was an Italian of the north of the Peninsula, who had been fond of fol-

---

[1] Business to-morrow.

lowing the chase on the slopes of the Apennines before chance had made him a courtier. He accepted the invitation with pleasure, and the party made the best of their way to the high ground now known as Arreton Downs.

"Ah!" said the Count, as he pointed northward to where the great Anderida Forest[1] might be seen stretching far beyond the range of sight, "there is the place for sport; a wilder country I have never seen, no, nor finer game. There are wild boars of which I have never seen the like in Italy, no, nor in the Hercynian Wood[2] itself, where I used to hunt years ago. Last year I killed one which measured six feet from snout to tail. There are wolves, too, and bears, and wild oxen; splendid fellows these last, as fierce as lions, and almost as big as elephants. But to-day we must be content with humbler sport."

This humbler game, however, afforded plenty of amusement, and they returned with a bag of eight fine hares—a very fair burden for the carrier of the game-bag—and an excellent appetite for dinner.

The meal, to which the Count had invited the captains of his galleys and the principal persons in

---

[1] The Forest of Anderida occupied a great part of Hampshire and nearly the whole of Sussex, except a strip of land along the coast. It must have measured a hundred miles from east to west.

[2] The Black Forest, part of which was known to the Romans.

the little colony which was now gathered about the villa, passed off very well. The young Italian was loud in his praises of everything. " Your oysters," he said, " all the world knows, but some of your other dishes are a surprise. The turbot, for instance, how incomparably superior to the flabby and taste-less things which they bring us from our own coasts. The colder water of the seas is, I suppose, the cause. The hares, too, how fine and fleshy ! You seem to be amazingly well off in the way of food in this corner of the world."

" Ah ! " said the Count, with a sigh, " we should do very well, if the rest of the world would only leave us alone. But our neighbours cannot be con-tent without a share of some of our good things, and they have a very rough and disagreeable way of asking for it."

The speaker went on to draw for the benefit of his guest a vivid picture of the trouble which the Saxons were giving by sea and the Picts by land, till the Italian exclaimed—

" Ah ! I see that you too have your disagreeables. I began to think that this was a land of peace and plenty, where one might find a pleasant refuge. But these barbarians, in one shape or another, are every-where. We are fallen upon evil times indeed."

" Yes," said the Count, " evil times, and no one knows how to deal with them ; and if God does send us a capable man, we treat him as if he were an enemy."

When the tables had been cleared, the Count rose and proposed the toast of the Emperor's health; but he did this without a single word of compliment, a significant omission that did not fail to attract the attention of all who were present. He then proceeded, and again without any preface, to read to the company the despatch which had been put into his hands the day before. It ran thus:

"*Flavius Honorius Augustus to the faithful and valiant Lucius Ælius, Count of the Saxon Shore, greeting.*

"*Our Imperial care for the dominions, which by Divine Providence have been committed to our trust, bids us combine the safety of the seat of our government with the welfare of the provinces. For, seeing that these are mutually related, as are the head and the limbs in the body of man, it is manifest that neither can prosper without the other. Our well-beloved and faithful province of Britain has now for many generations been protected by our invincible legions and fleets. But even as there comes a time when the most careful fathers judge it to be not only needless but even harmful to keep their children in dependence upon themselves, so do we now judge that our province may now with great advantage, not only to us— for of this we think little—but also to itself, defend itself*

The Count receiving the Letter of Honorius.

with its own resources. We charge you, therefore, our well-beloved and faithful Ælius, as having supreme command of the fleets of the said province of Britain, to withdraw them as soon as you conveniently may, but not without leaving our loyal subjects the assurance of our fatherly love and of the unfailing protection of our majesty. The Ever-Blessed Trinity keep and prosper both you and all that are committed to your charge. Given at Ravenna, the twelfth day before the Kalends of August,[1] in the year of our Lord 408, and the fifteenth year of our reign."

The reading of the despatch was followed by a dead silence. Every one had felt for some time that the present state of affairs could not last. Only a man of the vigorous character of the Count, and having long years of excellent service to fall back upon, could have maintained it so long, but it was impossible not to see that it must soon end. A solitary commander, without resources or support, could not maintain himself on the remotest borders of the Empire. Yet to know that the moment for the change had come was disturbing. The fleet, reduced as it had been to a petty squadron, was still, while it remained, the symbol of Imperial power, and seemed to be worth more in the way of protection than

---

[1] July 21st.

it really was. When this was withdrawn, Britain would be really left to itself; and this prospect, however it might be regarded elsewhere, was not agreeable to any one of the Count's guests.

The Count was the first to break the silence. "This," he said, "is manifestly a matter that calls for serious thought. Let us postpone it till to-morrow, and for the present turn ourselves to matters more suitable for a festive occasion. Perhaps my friend Claudian will give us the recitation of something with which he has already charmed the ears of our fellow-countrymen elsewhere."

The poet, not more reluctant than his brother-countryman to exhibit his genius, at once signified his willingness to comply with this request, and gave a recitation from an unfinished poem which he had then in hand. We may give a specimen, put into the best English that we can command—

> " The elemental order there she drew,
>   And Jove's high dwellings ; there you saw
> The needle tell how ancient Chaos grew
>   To harmony and law ;
>
> " How Nature set in order due and rank
>   Her atoms, raised the light on high,
> And to the middle place the weightier sank ;
>   There lustrous shone the sky,
>
> " The heavens were pink with flame, the ocean rolled,
>   The great world hung in mid suspense.
> Each was of diverse hue ; she worked in gold
>   The starry fires intense,

" Bade ocean flow in purple, and the shore
    With gems upraised.   Divinely wrought,
The threads embossed to swelling billows bore
    Strange likeness ; you had thought

" They dashed the seaweed on the rocks, or crept
    Hoarse murmuring thro' the thirsty sands.
Five zones, she added.   In mid place she kept
    With red distinct the lands

" Leaguered with burnings ; all the region showed
    Scorched into blackness, and the thread
Dry as with sunshine that eternal glowed ;
    Or either hand were spread

" The realms of life, lapt in a milder breath
    Kindly to men ; and next appear,
On this extreme and that, dull lands of death :
    She made them dark and drear

" With year-long frost, and saddened all the hue
    With endless winter ; last she showed
What seats her sire's grim brother holds ; nor knew
    The fated dark abode."[1]

---

[1] This is the translation of a passage from the first book of an unfinished poem by Claudian, entitled *De Raptu Proserpinæ*, " The Carrying off Proserpine."   It is an amplification of the legend that Pluto, god of the region of the dead, carried off Proserpine, daughter of Ceres, to be his wife and queen, while she was gathering flowers in the fields of Enna in Sicily.   The passage translated occurs in the first book, and describes the tapestry with which Proserpine is busy, as a gift to her absent mother.   The poem breaks off in the third book, while relating the search which the mother makes for her lost daughter.

CHAPTER XXV.

CONSULTATION.

THE next morning the Count invited the Imperial messenger to a private conference. His daughter and Carna were present, as was also Claudian.

"You have the latest news," the Count began. " Pray let us have them. Here we know nothing. But tell us first how you got here. It was noticed that you did not hoist the standard till you were within the Haven. You did not, I suppose, think it a safe flag to sail under."

"Well," replied the messenger, "I thought it better to have no flag at all. But, to tell the truth, the Labarum is not just now exactly the best passport in the world."

"You crossed from Gaul, I suppose ?" the Count went on. "How are matters there ?"

"Constantine, with the legions he brought from here, and those that have joined him since, is pretty well master of the country, and of Spain too."

"And what is the Emperor doing? Did he let these provinces go without a struggle? Spain was the first province that Rome ever had, and Gaul was the second. None, I take it, have been so steadily profitable, and now we are to lose them."

He rose from his seat, and walked up and down the room in an agitation which he could not conceal.

"And the only man who could keep the Empire together is gone; butchered, as if he were a criminal!"

The messenger said nothing to this outburst. He went on, "I believe his Majesty proposes to admit Constantine to a share of the Imperial honours, to make him Cæsar of Gaul and Spain."

"What!" said the Count. "Do not my ears deceive me? This fellow, whom I have seen wearing the collar for the neglect of duty, recognized as his colleague by Augustus!"[1]

"I do not pretend to know his Majesty's purposes, I can only say what is reported at head-quarters, and, it would seem, on good authority. But," continued the speaker, in a voice from which he had studiously banished all kind of emphasis, and looking as he spoke at the ceiling of the room, "your lordship is aware that the honours thus unexpectedly bestowed do not always turn out to the advantage of those who receive them."

---

[1] This was actually done about this time, and with the result foreshadowed in the conversation given above.

" What do you mean ? " asked the Count.

"I mean that what is given may be taken away— and taken away with very handsome interest for the loan—when the proper time comes. Your lordship has not forgotten the name of Carausius." [1]

" Well," said the Count, " this is not the old way Rome had of dealing with her enemies. But, ' other times, other manners.' Tell me now, if the Augustus has arranged or is going to arrange with Constantine, what about Alaric ? "

"Oh! he will be quiet for a time, or should be, if there is any truth in a barbarian's oath. You have heard how he marched on Rome ? "

" No, indeed," replied the Count. " I have heard nothing here, except, quite early in the year, a vague rumour that he was on the move again. But tell me—has Augustus given *him*, too, a share in the Empire ? "

"Not exactly ; but I will tell what has taken place. He marched on Rome."

---

[1] Carausius had held, towards the end of the third century, the same command as that of the Count of the Saxon Shore, had rebelled against the Emperor, made himself master of Britain and all the Western Seas, and had then proclaimed himself Augustus. The Emperor Diocletian made several attempts to reduce him, but, finding that this could not be done, acknowledged him as a partner in the Empire. Six years later Carausius was murdered by one of his lieutenants, Allectus, who doubtless hoped thus to bring himself into favour at Rome.

"Yes," interjected the Count, "and there was no Stilicho to save it!"

"The city was almost helpless. Even the walls had not been kept in repair, and if they had, there was no proper force to man them. The only thing possible was to make peace on the best terms that they could. I happened to be in Alaric's camp with a letter, under a flag of truce, the very day that the ambassadors came out to treat with the king, and I saw the whole affair. I don't mind saying that it was not one to make a man feel proud of being a Roman. The barbarians, it seemed to me, had not only all the strength on their side, but the dignity also. Alaric himself is a splendid specimen of humanity, every inch a king, the tallest and handsomest man in his army, and that, too, an army of giants. It was a contrast, I can tell you, between him and the two miserable, pettifogging creatures that represented the Senate. At first they tried what a little brag could do. 'Give us an honourable peace,' said their spokesman, 'or you will repent of having driven to despair a nation of warriors, a nation that has conquered the world.' The king laughed; he knew what the Romans have come to. 'The thicker the hay,' he said, 'the easier to mow.' And then he fixed the ransom that he would take for retiring from before the walls. Brennus throwing his sword into the scales was moderation in comparison to him. 'Give me,' he said, 'all the gold and silver, coined or un-coined, private property or public that you have, and all the other property that the envoys whom I shall send think worth taking; and hand over to me all the slaves that you have of the nations of the North, Goths, or Huns, or Vandals. You are pleased to call them barbarians, but they are more fit to be masters than you; and I will not suffer them to be in a bond-age so unworthy. Your Greeks, and Africans, and Asiatics, and such like cattle you may keep.' The ambassadors were pale with dismay. If they had taken back such an answer, the Romans had at least enough spirit left to tear them in pieces. 'What do you leave us, then?' they said. 'Your lives!' he thundered out. In the end, however, he softened somewhat. Five thousand pounds of gold and thirty thousand pounds of silver, and I don't know how much silk, and cloth, and spices, were what he finally asked. I know the city was stripped pretty bare before the Senate could make up the sum. I am told that the treasuries of the churches had to be emptied. Well, as I said, Alaric, if he keeps his bargain, ought to be quiet for a time, but you will see that the Emperor has need of all his friends round him, and all the strength which he can bring together. That is what I have to say by way of explanation of the despatch that I brought."

"May I ask you to leave us for a while?" said the Count to the young Italian.

When he had left the room the Count turned to his daughter, and said—

"And this is our country! This is Rome! The Emperor, forsooth, has need of all his friends. His friends indeed! I little thought that the day would come when I should feel ashamed of the title. But tell me, daughter; what shall we do? Shall we go?"

"What else can we do?" asked the girl.

"I have thought much about the matter since I heard the dreadful news of Stilicho's death, and have had all kinds of wild schemes in my head. I have felt that I could not go back and touch in friendship the hands that murdered him. Sometimes I thought, while Cedric was here, that we would take him with us, and sail eastward. I have had many a hard fight with these Saxons, but at least they are men, and brave men, too, who are true to their friends, if they hate their enemies. But that is now at an end. But is there no other way to go? What say you, Claudian —have you any counsel to give us?"

"I would not advise you to sail eastward," said the poet. "We know pretty well what lies that way; tribes of barbarians, of whom the less we see the better, with all respect to your friend Cedric, who seems to have been a fine fellow. But why not westward? You will laugh at me for believing in the Islands of the Blest. Well, I do not mean to say that there is a country where Achilles and the rest of the heroes are living in immortal joy and peace. If there is, it is not one which any ship, built by the art of man, can reach. But I do believe that there is a country. These old tales, depend upon it, have something more in them than mere fancy. Why, my lord, should not you be the one to find it ? "

" Yes, let us go, dear father," said Ælia, " and leave this dreadful world with all its troubles and quarrels behind us. Don't you think so, Carna ? "

Carna only smiled sadly.

" Or," continued the poet, " there is the land beyond the north, the country of the blessed Hyperboreans, that old Herodotus talks about. Why should we not go there ? Or, if that sounds too wild, there is Africa, with regions rich and fertile beyond all doubt that are waiting to be explored. These at least are no matter of legend. We know where they are. Let us search for them. Whatever world we may find, it can hardly be worse than that which we are leaving behind."

" And what says Carna ? " said the Count, turning, with an affectionate look, to his adopted daughter.

The girl thus appealed to flushed painfully. For a moment she seemed about to speak, but not a syllable passed her lips.

" Speak," cried the Count ; " you always see clearer and farther than the rest of us."

" My father," the girl went on, " I will speak from my heart, as I know you always wish me to do. Forgive me if I seem to teach when it is my part to learn and to obey.   But, if you ask what I think you should do, I say, ' Go home to Rome or Ravenna, or wherever else the Emperor bids you.'   After all, it is your country, and it never needed the help of good and brave men more than it does now."

" By heaven ! Claudian," cried the Count, after a brief silence, " the girl is right, as she always is. These are not the times for an honest man to turn his back upon his country. If I could reach the Islands of the Blest, or the happy people who live beyond the north, as easily as I can walk across this room, I would not do it ; and after all, what is the world without Rome to a Roman ? What say you, Claudian ? "

" I am but a poor singer, who has lost all that made him sing. I could do little in any case, and I doubt whether those who killed Stilicho will have anything but the axe for Stilicho's friend. Still, I go with you. It is not for a Roman to say that Rome is unworthy."

" So that is settled," exclaimed the Count.

" Oh, Carna," cried Ælia, throwing her arms round her sister, " shall we ever be as happy again as we have been in this dear place ? "

Carna clung to her, and sobbed as if her heart would break.

"Does it trouble you so much to go ? " asked the Count. " Surely the place is not so much to you. You can be happy, wherever you may be, with those you love."

The girl lifted up a tear-stained face to him.

" Father," she said—" more than father, for you have loved me without any tie of kindred—I cannot go, my home is here."

" Nay, child, what are you saying ? Your home has been with us ever since you were a babe in arms, and it is so still ; or," he added, with a smile, " are you going to leave us for a husband ? "

The girl blushed crimson as she shook her head. When she could recover her speech, choked, as it was, with sobs, she said—

" You asked me just now what you should do, and I said ' Go home to your country.' Can I do less myself ? Rome is your country, and Britain is mine. And oh, if Rome wants all her sons and daughters, how much more does this poor Britain ! "

" But where will you live ? " broke in the Count's daughter; " Where will you be safe ? Think of the dreadful things you have gone through within the last few months ! How can you bear to face them with your friends gone ? And, dearest Carna," she went on, as she clasped her still closer, " how can I live without you ? "

" My dearest sister," sobbed the girl, " don't make

it harder than it is. It breaks my heart to part from you, but I cannot doubt what my duty is. And I am not without hope. There are brave men here, and men who love their country, and I cannot but trust that they will be able to do something. Of course, we shall stumble, for we have not been used to go alone, but I do hope that we shall not fall altogether."

"But, Carna, what can you do?" said Ælia. "You seem to be sacrificing yourself for nothing."

"Not for nothing; it is something if I can only sit at home and pray. But it must be at home that I must pray. God would not hear me if I were to put myself in some safe, comfortable place, and then pretend to care for the poor people whom I had left behind."

She hurried from the room when she had said this, as if she could not trust herself against persuasions that touched her heart so nearly.

"Carna is right," said the Count, when she had gone, "but I feel as if she were going to her death."

CHAPTER XXVI.

FAREWELL!

THE resolution to return to Italy once made, the Count lost no time in carrying it out. His own preparations for departure did not cost him much trouble. He began by offering freedom to all the slaves in his household. The difficulty was in inducing them to accept it. So kind a master had he been—in spite of an occasional outburst of temper—and so uncertain were the prospects of a quiet life in Britain, that very few felt any eagerness to be independent, and the boon had to be forced upon them or made acceptable by a considerable bribe. With the free population that since the departure of the legions had gathered in increasing numbers about the villa it was still more difficult to deal. Many of them were quite helpless people whom it seemed equally difficult to take and to leave behind. To all that were of Italian birth, or that had kinsfolk or friends on the Continent who might be reasonably expected to give them a home, the Count offered a passage. For others employment was found in Londinium and other towns. But, when all that was possible had been done, there was a helpless remnant, about whom the Count felt much as the occupants of the last boat must feel at the sight of the poor creatures whom they are forced to leave behind on a sinking ship.

Carna had quitted the villa very soon after her resolution to remain in Britain had been made. It was indeed too painful to remain there, for, though the Count had confessed that she was right, his daughter remained unconvinced, and assailed her with incessant entreaties and reproaches which went very near to breaking her heart. She made her home with the old priest whose wife was a distant kinswoman of her own, and found, as such tender hearts always will, a solace for her own sorrows in relieving the troubles of others.

About the middle of September all was ready for a start. The two serviceable ships that were left to the Count were loaded to their utmost capacity with the persons and property of the departing colony. Their sailing masters had indeed remonstrated as strongly as they dared.

" We *may* get safely across," said the senior of them, " if all goes better than we have any right to expect. But if it comes on to blow we shall hardly be able to handle our ships ; and if we meet with the pirates—well, a man might as well go into battle with his hands tied."

The Count refused to listen to these protests. Even the suggestion that the cargo should be divided, and part left for a second voyage he scouted, " It will not do," he said, " the poor people would fancy they were being left behind, and I am not at all sure that they would not be right. It is only too likely that if we once get to the other side we should *not* come back. No! we will sink or swim together."

About an hour before noon on the fifteenth of the month, the crews were ready to weigh anchor. The Count and his daughter, who had just taken their last view of the villa which had been their home for so many years, were standing on the little jetty, ready to step into the boat that was to convey them to the ship. Carna and the old priest and his wife were with them, and the hour of farewell had come. Ælia, if she had not reconciled herself to separation from her sister, at least saw that it was inevitable, and was resolved not to make the parting bitterer than it must needs be. She affected a cheerfulness which she did not feel.

" Good-bye, Carna," she cried, throwing her arms round the girl's neck. " Good-bye! now we are going like swallows in the autumn, and very likely shall come back like them in the spring. Meanwhile keep the nest as warm for us as you can."

"Remember, Carna," said the Count, "that you have a home as long as either I or my daughter have a roof over our heads. You are doing your duty in staying, but there is a limit even to duty. As long as you can be of service, stop; I would not have it otherwise; but don't sacrifice yourself and those that love you for nothing."

Carna's heart was too full to let her speak. She caught the Count's hands and kissed them. Then she turned to Ælia, and taking her gold cross and chain — the only ornament that she wore — hung it round her sister's neck. When she had succeeded in choking down her sobs, she whispered, "Take this, and, if you will give me yours, we will bear each other's crosses, and, perhaps, they will be a little lighter. But oh, how heavy!"

"Kneel, my children," said the old priest, and the little group knelt down, while the rowers in the boat uncovered their heads. After repeating the paternoster and a few simple words of prayer, he raised his hand and blessed them, then fell on his knees beside them. After two or three minutes of silent supplication the Count rose, and almost lifted his daughter into the boat, so broken down was she with the passion of her grief. Carna remained on her knees, her face buried in her hands. To have looked up and seen father and sister go was more than she dared to do. For the struggle that she fancied was over had begun again in her heart, and she could not feel sure even then that duty would prevail. The Count gently laid his hand upon her head and blessed her, then stepped into the boat. As the rowers dipped their oars in the water, a gleam of sunshine burst through the clouds, and lighted as with a glory the head of the kneeling girl.

CHAPTER XXVII.

MARTIANUS.

THE little community that remained in the neighbourhood of the villa after the departure of the
Count and his household had plenty to occupy their
thoughts and hands. The Count had behaved with
a liberality and a discretion that were both equally
characteristic of him. All the stock of what may be
called the home farm, all the agricultural implements,
the cattle, sheep, and pigs, and as much of the stores
of corn that he could spare, he had made over to the
priest and two other principal persons in the settlement for the benefit of the community at large.
This was an excellent start, and removed all immediate anxiety for the future. The stores of provisions
had been increased by opportune purchases before
the resolution to go had been taken, and enough was
left to last, if managed with due economy, over the
coming winter.

Carna found plenty of employment of the kind in

which she found her greatest pleasure. There was indeed a terrible gap in her life; not only had she lost those whom she had loved all her life as father and sister, but her intellectual interests had dropped away from her. Many of the books at the villa had indeed been left with her, but then there was no one to whom to talk about them. The old priest never opened a volume except it was a service book; his wife could not even read. But the time never hung heavily upon her hands, for there was plenty of work to do among the sick and sorry. As the autumn went on an epidemic, which a modern doctor would probably have described as measles, broke out among the children, and Carna spent her days and nights in ministering to the little sufferers. The one relief that she allowed herself—and there was no little sadness mixed with the pleasure which it gave her—was to spend an hour, when she could snatch one from her many cares, in the deserted rooms of the villa. The indulgence was rare, not only because her leisure was infrequent, but because she was conscious of feeling somewhat relaxed after it for the effort of her daily life ; but when it came it was precious. Not a room, not a picture on the walls, not a pattern in the tesselated pavements, that did not call up a hundred associations, and make the past in which she had enjoyed so much happiness live again in her fancy. The dwelling was under the charge of an old couple, who gladly kept it clean in exchange for the shelter of two or three of the rooms, and Carna was free to wander about it as she would, while she felt a certain security in the knowledge that the place was not wholly deserted.

The autumn and winter passed without any incident of importance. News from the Continent had never been very regular during that season of the year, and now it came only at the rarest intervals. All that the settlement heard went to show that there was but little chance of the return of the legions. Constantine, after some changes of fortune, had made himself master of Gaul and Spain, and had established a kingdom which looked so much as if it might last, that he had been regularly acknowledged by Honorius as a partner in the Empire. But it would be long before he could spare money or men for adding Britain to his dominions. From Britain itself the news was mostly of the most dismal kind. The Picts, indeed, were not as troublesome as usual. Happily for their neighbours on the south, their attention had been occupied by the tribes on the north, who had been driven by a season of unusual scarcity to forage for themselves. The robbers, in fact, had been obliged to defend themselves against being robbed, and Britain had had in consequence a quiet time. But the people used it to quarrel among themselves. There were scores of chiefs who had each his pedigree, by which he traced his lineage to some king of the pre-Roman days, and which gave him, he fancied, a title to rule over his neighbours. And besides these personal jealousies, there was a great division which split the nation into two hostile factions. There were Britons, who held to Roman ways, and among them, to the religion which Rome had given, and there were Britons who looked back to the old independent days, and to the faith which their fore-fathers had held long before the name of Christ had been heard out of or in the land of His birth. The former party was by far the more numerous, but its adherents were those who had suffered most by Britain's four centuries of servitude ; in the latter the virtues of freedom had been kept alive by a carefully cherished tradition. They were few in number; but they were vigorous and enthusiastic, even fanatical. It was clear that this strife within would cause at least as much trouble as would come from enemies without.

It was about seven months after the Count's departure when Carna paid one of her customary visits to the villa. She had been unusually busy for three or four weeks previously, and had not found time to come. As she passed through the garden, on her way to the house, she noticed that the place looked somewhat neater and less neglected than usual. This, however, did not surprise her, as she had gently remonstrated with the old keeper for doing so little, and, in her usual kindly way, had followed up her reproof with a little present. Accordingly she passed on without thinking more of the matter to the little sitting-room which she had once shared with Ælia, and prepared to spend an hour of quiet enjoyment with a book. Her books, indeed, she kept for these visits to the villa. Not only was her time elsewhere closely occupied, but her hostess, kindly and affectionate as she generally was, could not conceal her dislike of the volumes which Carna loved so dearly.

In the midst of her reading she was startled by the unaccustomed sound of footsteps. She lifted her eyes from the page and saw a sight so unexpected that for a few moments she could not collect her thoughts or believe her eyes.

The British chief Martianus stood before her.

She had seen him last at the Great Temple, and the recollections of those days and nights of horror, her capture, her hurried journey, and the interrupted sacrifice, crowded upon her, and almost overpowered her. Nor could she help giving one thought to the question—if this man's presence recalls such horrors in the past, what does it not mean for the future? Still, the courage which had supported her so bravely before did not fail her now. She rose from her seat and calmly faced the intruder, while she waited for him to speak.

Martianus began in a tone of the deepest respect. "Lady, I am truly glad that you condescend to honour this poor house of mine with your presence."

"This house of yours!" repeated the girl, with astonishment.

"Lady, doubtless you do not know that this villa was built by its former owner on land which belonged to my family, and which was taken from them by force. I do not speak of the Count—he was too honourable a man to do anything of the kind—I speak of the former owner, or so-called owner, from whom he purchased it. In the Count's time I said nothing of my claim. I would not have troubled him for the world. But now that he has gone, and practically given up the place, I am justified, I think, in asserting my ownership."

"I know nothing of these matters," said Carna, coldly, "but I will take care not to intrude again."

"Intrusion!" said the chief. "Did I not say that there is no one who would be more welcome here? We were friends once, in the good Count's time; why should we not be so again? and more," he added in a whisper.

"Friends with you! Surely that is impossible. You cannot wish it yourself, after what has happened. You seem to forget."

"Lady, Carna—I used to call you Carna when you were a child—I do try to forget that dreadful

CARNA AND MARTIANUS.

night. I was overborne by those double-dyed villains, Carausius and Ambiorix. Believe me, it was
against my will that I took any part in that dreadful
business. And you will remember I never lifted a
hand against you, no, nor against that base champion
of yours. You will do me that justice. Carausius,
thank Heaven! has got his deserts, and I have
broken with Ambiorix."

Carna remained silent.

Martianus resolved to try another appeal, and,
presuming that the girl's recollections of the scene
might be confused by fear, did not scruple to depart
considerably from the truth.

"I implore you to believe that I could not have
allowed that horrible deed to be accomplished. If
that base fellow who had the privilege of saving
you had not appeared, I was ready myself to interfere. I know that I ought to have done so before;
it has been a ceaseless regret to me that I did
not. But I wanted to keep on terms with those two,
and I held back till the last moment. Forgive me
my irresolution, Carna, but do not believe that I
could have been one of the murderers."

The girl's recollections of the scene, which were
quite free from the confusion which Martianus had
imagined, did not agree with this account of his
behaviour, but she did not think it worth while to
argue the point.

" Let it be as you will," she said, with a cold dignity, "but you can imagine that these recollections are not pleasing to me. And now I will bid you farewell."

She stepped forward as she spoke with the intention of at once leaving the room, but Martianus barred the way. Dropping on one knee, he caught her hand. For a moment Carna, who had still something of the child in her, felt a strong impulse to use the hand that was still free in dealing him a vigorous blow. But her womanly dignity prevailed: she only wrenched her hand away with something like violence. There was something in the foppish appearance and insincere manner of Martianus that set her more decidedly against him than even the recollection of the plot in which he had been concerned.

" I will listen to what you have to say, but do not touch me."

" You give me little encouragement," Martianus began, " but still I will speak. I say nothing about myself, only about my country—your country and mine. I know how you love it. We have all heard what sacrifices you have made for it, how you gave up home and friends sooner than leave it. Make, if I must put it so, one sacrifice more. You are the heiress of the great Caradoc, the noblest king that Britain ever had, whom even the Romans were compelled to admire. I can reckon among my ancestors Cunobelin. Apart our claims might be disputed; together they will make a title which no one can dispute to the crown of Britain. Yes, Carna, it is nothing less than that—the crown of Britain that is in question."

"A crown does not tempt me," said Carna, looking the speaker straight in the face.

"Ah! it is not that," replied the suitor; "you mistake me. I never dreamed of tempting you. I know only too well that it would be impossible. But think what a British crown really means. It means a united Britain, strong against the Picts, strong against the Saxons; and without it—think what that would mean. Every tribe—for we should split up into tribes again—for itself; every chief working for his own hand; the Picts plundering the inland, the Saxons harrying the coast. Oh, Carna! as you love your country—I don't speak of myself, though that, too, might come in time, if a man's devotion is of any avail—but if you love your country, do not say no."

It was a powerful appeal, and touched Carna's heart at the point where it was most accessible. And she was so candid and transparent a soul that what she felt in her heart she soon showed in her face.

Martianus saw his advantage, **but,** happily for

Carna, did not press it as he might have done. The fact was that he **was** so conscious of his own insincerity and falsehood that his courage failed him, and he dared not press his suit any further. Had he gone on, he might have entangled the girl in a promise which her feeling for truth would not have permitted her to break, which would have made her even shut her eyes to the truth. As it was, he thought it his best policy to rest content with the progress that he had made. He raised Carna's hand respectfully to his lips, and, with a low salutation, opened the door.

CHAPTER XXVIII.

A RIVAL.

IT was a fact that Martianus had taken possession
of the villa in the island, on the strength of a claim
which was far less definite than he had chosen to
represent to Carna.   But no other owner was forthcoming, and the place was important in the minds
of the British population as having been the dwelling
of the last representative of Roman power.   The
new occupant might seem to have succeeded to the
position of the one who had lately quitted it.   It
flattered the man's vanity, too, to put himself in the
place, so to speak, of the powerful Count of the
Shore, while he could use the appliances of the villa,
which were comfortable and even luxurious, to gratify
his taste for what he called the pleasures of civilized
life.   His establishment would probably have failed
to satisfy the fastidious taste of a Roman gentleman;
the cooking was barbarous, and the service generally
rude.   Still there was a certain imitation, which im-

posed at least upon the ignorant, of Roman refinement, and Martianus flattered himself that he was
at least a passable successor of Count Ælius.

Meanwhile he pursued his suit to Carna with a
good deal of craft. He was a diligent attendant
at the village church, and professed to feel such an
interest in the teaching of the old priest that the
ministrations in church must be supplemented by
conversations at home. To Carna he said little or
nothing about his personal claims, but he was
eloquent on the subject of the future of Britain.
About this she was never tired of hearing, and in
hearing him speak of it, which he did with a certain
eloquence, the sense of his falseness and unreality
began to grow fainter in her mind. The maiden
faith which "glorifies clown and satyr" began to
make this schemer, who indeed was not without
ability and accomplishments, look like a genuine
patriot. As for the priest and his wife, they were
simply captivated by him, and never lost an opportunity of praising him to their young kinswoman.
On the whole, his suit made some progress. It was
only when he seemed to put forward any personal
claim, or ventured to address to Carna any personal
compliments, that she decidedly shrank from him.
He was quite shrewd enough to see this, and though
it was a very unpleasant experience for his vanity as
well as for his love, he did not fail to guide his con-

duct by it. As long as he talked about Britain, its wrongs in the past, and its hopes for the future, he was sure of a favourable hearing.

Martianus had other things to think of besides his suit to Carna. As he said, he had broken entirely with Ambiorix. He had found that the strength of the old Druid party had been greatly exaggerated, and that in fact the time for its revival had gone by for ever. Any chance, too, of even temporary success that it might have had had been lost with the life of Carausius. The priest had held many threads of secret intrigue in his hands, and there was no one to take them up, when they dropped from his hand. And Ambiorix, besides being worth but little as an ally, had wanted too much, for he was not of a temper to be satisfied with the second place.

Still Martianus was well aware that his rival would have to be reckoned with sooner or later. If he could induce Carna to become his wife, and thus unite her family claim to his own, this reckoning might be got through with care and success. If he had to rely upon himself the chances would be decidedly less favourable. The dilemma in which he found himself was this. On the one hand, to hasten his suit might be to ruin it altogether; Carna, too, might fairly ask him for something more substantial than his own assertion of his pretensions. On the other hand, there was the danger of being attacked and crushed before he could make his appeal to the country. Ambiorix, he knew, was a man of even desperate courage, and would not suffer himself to be effaced without a struggle.

Martianus did his best to guard himself against this danger. He strengthened the fortifications which the Count had made round the villa, laid up a store of provisions which might be sufficient for a prolonged siege, and used all his resources—he was one of the richest men in Britain—to get together as large and effective a garrison as possible.

These precautions were not taken a day too soon. About the beginning of June he received intelligence from his agents on the mainland that Ambiorix was preparing to attack him. He hurried at once with the news to the priest's house.

"You know," he said, "that my house has always been at your disposal, but, much as I should have liked to receive you as my guests, I would not press the invitation upon you. But now, in the face of what I have just heard, your coming is a necessity. Ambiorix and his followers are almost on the way to attack us, and there is no place of safety but the villa."

The proposition was most distasteful to Carna, who shuddered at the thought of entering her old home in such society. At first she was disposed to be generally incredulous, knowing that Martianus was not incapable of exaggerating, and even of inventing, when he had an object to serve. Compelled, by the proofs which the chief advanced, to acknowledge that the danger was real, she took refuge in the argument that "it did not concern them."

"We are too insignificant to be harmed," she said.

"Pardon me, Carna," replied Martianus. "You surely know better than that about yourself. And if, as I can easily believe, you are careless on your own account, think of your host. There is nothing that Ambiorix hates with so deadly a hatred as a Christian priest."

The old priest, a worthy man, but not of the stuff of which martyrs are made, was terribly alarmed at this statement. Carna, too, was compelled to acknowledge that this fear was not without reason, and reluctantly consented to the removal. Her mind once made up, she found abundance of occupation in making it as little grievous to others as might be. The villa could not hold any great number of inmates in addition to the garrison, and of course it was necessary that the number of non-combatants should be as small as possible. Some of the inhabitants of the settlement could, of course, remain safely in their homes. They had little or nothing to be robbed of, and the expected assailants had no other reason for harming them. But many households had to be broken up, and as only very few could be received at the villa, there were many painful scenes to be gone through, and Carna was unceasingly busy giving all the comfort and help that she could. Martianus, who was not unkindly in temper, put all his resources at her disposal, and his readiness to assist put him higher in her favour than he had ever been before.

Nor was she sorry that she had found shelter within the fortifications of the villa when the next morning revealed the presence of the invaders. They had come across in the night to the number of several hundreds, and could be seen from the windows of the villa. And a very singular sight they were. A spectator might have imagined himself to have been carried back more than four centuries and a half, and to be looking on the hosts which had gathered to oppose the landing of the first Cæsar. These warriors who came up shouting to the palisade which formed the outer defence of the villa seemed to be absolute barbarians; no one could have believed that for many generations they had been subjects of a civilized power. They had, in fact, deliberately thrown off all the signs of that subjection. It was the dream of Ambiorix to have Britain such as she might have been had Rome never conquered her. It was a hopeless attempt, this rolling back the course of time by four centuries, but in such matters as dress and equipment something could be done. Accordingly, his troops were such as the troops of Cassibelan might have been had they suddenly risen from their graves. Most of them were naked to the waist; what clothing they had was chiefly of skins, though some wore gaily-coloured trews. All wore their hair falling over their shoulders, and long, drooping moustaches, but no beard or whisker. All the exposed parts of their bodies were dyed a deep indigo-blue, by the application of woad. Ambiorix had been very anxious to revive the chariots of his ancestors, but had been compelled to give up the idea. In any case he could not have transported them to the island. He had been at great pains to instruct them in the genuine British war-cries, as far as tradition had preserved them. Here, again, the result had been somewhat disappointing. There were things which they had learnt from Rome which they could not put off as easily as their dress; and the challenges which they shouted out to the besieged as they surged up to the defences were a curious mixture of the British and Latin tongues.

The battle at first went decidedly against the assailants. The Count had left behind him a catapult among other effects which he had not thought it worth while to remove; and Martianus, who had practised some of the garrison in the use of it, brought it inot play with considerable effect. The very first discharge killed one of the lesser chiefs, and a little later in the day Ambiorix himself was badly bruised by one of the stones propelled from it. Meanwhile the defenders escaped almost wholly without injury. There was no need for them to leave the shelter of the buildings. As long as they kept within this the bows and slings of the enemy failed to harm them. One or two rash young recruits exposed themselves unnecessarily, and were wounded in consequence; but when Ambiorix, about an hour before sunset, called off his men, the garrison found that the casualties had been very slight and few.

During the night the besiegers were not idle. They constructed a mantelet [1] of wicker work covered with stout hides, and brought it out close to the palisade—an operation which the besieged, with a culpable carelessness, allowed them to do unmolested. From under cover of this they plied long poles, armed at the ends with blades of steel (for Ambiorix was not so obstinate a conservative as to go back to the axe of bronze), and hacked away at the palisade. The catapult produced no effect on this erection, and though arrows, discharged almost perpendicularly into the air so as to fall just

---

[1] Mantelet : a shield of wood, metal, or rope, for the protection of sappers, &c.

on the other side of it, inflicted some injury, the work went on without interruption. Martianus, seeing this, headed a sally in person, and, after a sharp struggle, succeeded in possessing himself of it. The wicker work was broken in pieces, and the hides carried off within the line of defences.

The next three days passed without incident, and the inmates of the villa began to hope that the danger had passed over. In reality, however, the besiegers were collecting materials for the construction of another mantelet on a much larger scale. As much of this as was possible was put together out of sight of the villa, and on the morning of the fourth day an erection of considerable size could be seen about fifty yards from the palisade. It soon became evident that the new plan of the assailants was to try the effect of fire. Arrows were wrapped round with tow, and, when this had been lighted, were discharged into the enclosure. Some mischief was done, not so much to the buildings, for it was not difficult to put out the fire if the arrows happened to fall on an inflammable place, but to the garrison. The men who had to extinguish the flames could not avoid exposing themselves, and those who exposed themselves were frequently hit by the slingers and archers. On the whole, however, little progress was made, and when, in the course of the evening, a heavy rain came on, and the wind, which had hitherto assisted the flames, altogether died away, the discharge ceased.

It was now necessary for Ambiorix to bring matters to a crisis. His followers had nearly exhausted the store of provisions which they had brought with them, and, as he was unwilling to alienate the inhabitants of the island by resorting to plunder, he did not see how he could replenish it. Nothing remained, therefore, but to try a direct assault, and this he did in the early dawn of the sixth day after his arrival. Under cover of a heavy mist which rolled in from the sea, and helped by the neglect of the sentinels, who, never very watchful, had relaxed their care altogether when the light became visible, he brought his men close up to the palisade at the spot where an opening had been left, closed with a strong gate. For a few minutes, such was the supineness of the garrison, the assailants were allowed to batter and hew at this undisturbed. When some of the defenders had been rallied to the spot, the work was more than half done. Ambiorix, who was now entirely recovered from the injury received on the first day of the siege, plied his axe with extraordinary energy, and his immediate followers, whom he had carefully selected for their courage and strength, followed his example. By the time Martianus arrived on the scene the gate had been broken down, and the assailants were pouring into the enclosure.

The garrison, who were outnumbered in the proportion of nearly three to one, were at once ordered to
fall back into the quadrangle of the villa. They formed
a line across the open side where they were covered
by the archers and slingers posted on the roofs of
the various buildings. Here a long and fierce struggle ensued. The defenders had some advantage in
their position, and were better drilled and disciplined ;
the assailants, on the other hand, had the courage of
fanaticism. When an hour had passed, and the
combatants, by mutual consent, paused to take breath,
both sides had lost many in killed and wounded, but
neither had gained any considerable advantage.

Carna meanwhile had been busy ministering to the
needs of the wounded, and was scarcely aware of the
true position of affairs, the room in which she was at
work not commanding a view of the space in which
the struggle was going on. Chancing, however, to
leave it for a moment in search of something which
she wanted for her work, she saw what had taken
place. In a moment her resolution was taken.
During the siege her thoughts had been taken up, not
with the danger to herself and the other inmates of the
villa, but with the terrible fact that Britons were
fighting against Britons. Long before she would
have attempted to put an end to their cruel strife, if
she had seen any hope of success. She would not
have hesitated risking her life in the attempt. In-

deed she had proposed to Martianus that she should go with a party bearing a flag of truce, and seek an interview with the hostile commander. He had met her with a courteous and peremptory refusal, and she had been compelled to acquiesce. But now it seemed to her that her chance was come. Taking advantage of the pause in the struggle, she ran between the combatants, and threw herself on her knees with her face towards the assailants.

A murmur of astonishment and admiration ran through both the ranks. She seemed to be a visitor from another world, so strange, so unexpected, and, at the same time, so beautiful was her appearance.

"Britons, brothers," she cried, in a sweet but penetrating voice, which made itself heard through the throng, "what is this? Britons, brothers, have you forgotten what you are? Your masters have left you. You carry arms which have been forbidden to you for more than four hundred years, and must you first use them against your own countrymen? Have you no enemies abroad that you must look for them at home?"

A shriek of terror, followed by a wild war cry, which, thoughstr ange to many of the crowd, was only too familiar to the dwellers on the coast, gave a fearful emphasis to her words. The enemies from without were there.

CHAPTER XXIX.

AN UNEXPECTED ARRIVAL.

CEDRIC, after making good his escape from the villa, as has been related, had nearly died of hunger on the shore to which he had managed to make his way. When he was almost at his last gasp, a Saxon galley had touched at the very spot to supply itself with water. Fortunately for him it was commanded by a kinsman of his own, who persuaded the crew—the Saxon adventurers had to be dealt with by persuasion rather than by command—to return home with their passenger. This probably saved his life; his mother, a skilful leech, whose fame was spread abroad among the dwellers on the coast, nursed him back into health. Still he had suffered long and much; and it was not till the summer was far advanced that he was allowed to join an expedition. His noble birth, his reputation for strength and courage, not a little enhanced, of course, by his late escape, and the personal fascination that he exercised on all about him, pointed him out, young as he was, for command.

Carna had been unceasingly in his thoughts since the day when he had last seen her. During the delirium of his illness her name had been continually on his lips, and one of the earliest confidences of his recovery was the story of his love for this Christian maiden of the west. His mother was touched by the story. The girl's passionate desire for the welfare of the son that was dead (which she appreciated without comprehending its motive), and the very heroism which the son that was living had shown in defending her, combined to move her heart. That any living woman could resist the attraction of such a champion as her son, she did not believe for a moment, in spite of all that Cedric could say about the height of saintliness on which Carna stood; and by degrees the young chief himself found his worshipping devotion mingled with hopes that were very sweet to his heart.

It is not surprising, therefore, that as soon as he was at sea, and the destination of their voyage became a question, his thoughts at once turned to the island. Approaching it with caution, for he was too good a leader to risk an encounter with the superior force of the Roman squadron, he learnt with surprise that the Count had departed. Of Carna his informant, a fisherman who found it answer his purpose to give what information he could to the Saxons, could tell him nothing, and Cedric naturally supposed that she had gone with the family into which she had been adopted. The news struck a strange chill into his heart, but at the same time it relieved him of considerable perplexity. His course was now clear; if the Romans were gone there was nothing to be feared. He knew the approaches to the villa, and how weak were its defences, and he felt sure that a British garrison would not be a match for his own vigorous Saxons.

He reached the island two days after the landing of Ambiorix. Acting as his own spy on the strength of his knowledge of the country, he soon found out the position of affairs, and thought that he could not do better than wait to see how things would turn out. The galleys—Cedric had two under his command—lay in hiding at some little distance from the Haven, and meanwhile every detail of the struggle was watched, unknown to the combatants, by scouts who carried news of its progress to their chief. The gathering of the troops previous to the attack on the fortifications had been observed and rightly understood by these men. Cedric had been at once informed of what was in progress, had landed his crews, amounting in all to about two hundred, and marched with all the speed that was possible to the scene of action. As the news had reached him not long after midnight he was able to reach the spot very soon after the attack had commenced.

The battle-cry of the Saxons, terrible to those who knew it, scarcely less terrible, with its shrillness and fierceness, to those to whom it was strange, arrested the attention of all, and made every eye turn to the rear of the attacking party. There could be seen, running swiftly up the ascent which led to the palisade, the band of Saxons. In front a huge standard-bearer carried a blood-red banner, on which was wrought in black the raven of Odin. Behind him came, in a loose order which served to conceal their scanty number, Cedric's warriors, a sturdy race, whose tall stature was made to seem almost gigantic by the height to which their hair was dressed. They were formidable foes, but still there were brave men in both the British parties who would have had the courage to stand up against them. Unhappily one of the panics which defy all reason and all individual courage began among the inland Britons at the sight of these strange enemies; and, once begun, it could not be checked. Ambiorix, indeed, with a few of his immediate followers, faced the enemy, but was quickly swept away by the rush of their onset. Martianus, with some of the garrison, carrying Carna along with him, took refuge in the villa, and hastily secured the doors. Others fled wildly over the country, or hid themselves in the out-buildings. Nowhere was there any thought of resistance, and the Saxons won their victory almost without losing a drop of blood.

Cedric's eyes, sharpened as they were by love, had caught a glimpse of Carna, as she was swept in the throng of fugitives within the doors of the villa, and he at once led his men to the attack. Any defence of the place against assailants so determined would have been hopeless, even had the garrison been as resolute as they were, in fact, feeble and demoralized. A few sturdy blows from Cedric's battle-axe brought the principal door to the ground, and he rushed across the fragments into the hall, followed by some ten of his attendants. The rest he had signed to remain without. Carna, who, herself undismayed amidst all the tumult, was surrounded by a group of terrified men and women, stood facing him. The crimson mounted to her forehead as she met his eyes, for she saw, as no woman could fail to see, the love that was in them; but she showed no other sign of emotion.

"Spare these poor creatures," she said, pointing to her terrified companions.

"Your lives are safe," said Cedric in British. "Go with this man, and he pointed to one of his attendants, to whom at the same time he gave some brief directions. He turned to Carna : "Lady," he said, "this is no time for many words; and I could not say them if it were, for my tongue is ill-taught in your language. But you cannot have failed to see my heart.   It is yours, and all that I have.   Come and be a queen in my home and among my people."

The girl's eyes, which she had turned to the ground at his first address, were now lifted to meet his gaze.   " I cannot leave my people," she said.

" Yet," he answered, " the good women of whom you used to tell me, whose lives are written in that holy book of yours, left their own people to follow their husbands."

" Yes, but the God of the husbands whom they followed was the God whom they worshipped in their own homes.   You worship strange gods, with whom I can have no fellowship."

" Come with me and teach the truth to my people and me," cried the young man, feeling that there was nothing which he would not do to win this bright, brave, beautiful maiden.

" Listen, Cedric," she answered—it was the first time that she had called him by his name, and he thought that he had never known before what a name it was—" You told me some time since that you would sooner go into the everlasting darkness with your own people than bow the knee to a God whom you believed to have dealt unjustly with them.   It was a noble resolve ; and I have honoured you for it.   Will you give it up for the love of a woman ? If you did, I could honour you no more, and you are too good to have a wife that did not honour you.   No, Cedric, I will pray for you. Perhaps God will hear me, and give you light, and bring us together to the blessed Christ, but it cannot be here."

She caught his right hand which he had reached out in the earnestness of his speaking, and lifted it to her lips. Her kiss was the last expression of her gratitude. And perhaps there was something in it of a woman's love. But she never faltered for one instant in the resolve that was to separate them.

Behind Cedric stood a burly, middle-aged warrior, his father's foster-brother. He had watched the scene with an intense interest, and though of course he could not understand what was said, had a very shrewd notion of the turn which affairs were taking. Perhaps he saw, too, expressed in the girl's tone something of a feeling which the young man was too rapt in his adoration to observe. Anyhow, he was ill-content that his young chief should miss the bride on whom his heart was set, and who seemed so worthy of him.

"A noble maiden!" he whispered to Cedric, "and fit to be the wife and mother of kings; and I think that she loves you. Shall we carry her off? I warrant that it will not be long before she forgives us."

"Peace!" said Cedric, turning fiercely upon him, "Peace! Would you have me wed a slave? My wife must come to me freely, or come not at all."

He spoke to Carna again. " Your will is my law. If you say that we must part, I go. But, lady, you must leave this house. My people are set upon burning it, and I could not hinder them, if I would."

Without another word, she obeyed his bidding, and passed into the court, followed by Cedric and his attendants.

Meanwhile some of the Saxon crews had been busy with their torches, and the flames were beginning to gain a mastery over the building. Before many minutes had passed the sheds and outbuildings, which were, to a great extent, constructed of wood, were in a blaze, while dense volumes of smoke rolled out of the windows of the villa itself. Carna stood spellbound by the sight, at once so terrible and so grand. The spectacle of a burning house exercises a curious fascination even on those for whom it means loss and disaster, and Carna, even in that supreme crisis of her life, could not help gazing at the conflagration, and even admiring unconsciously the splendid contrasts of light and darkness which it produced.

It seemed as if that day was about to sweep away all her past. She had torn from her heart her half-acknowledged love ; she saw the home of her childhood and youth vanishing into smoke and ashes ; and now another actor in the bygone of her life was to disappear for ever.

Martianus had observed the scene from the chamber in which he had taken refuge, and had misunderstood it. He fancied that the girl, whom, though no formal betrothal had bound her to him, he regarded as his own, was going of her own accord with this Saxon robber, in whom, of course, he recognized the champion who had saved her life at the Great Temple. The thought stung him to madness. With all his foppery and frivolity, he had the courage of his race. He might probably have escaped unnoticed from the burning building. But, disdaining flight, he rushed at Cedric, heedless of the odds which he was challenging.

The chief's followers, knowing their master's temper, stood aside to let the conflict be decided without their interference. It was fierce, but it was brief. Martianus was a skilled swordsman, but a life of indolence, if not of excess, had slackened his sinews and unsteadied his nerves. He parried some of his antagonist's blows with sufficient adroitness, but his defence grew weaker and weaker, and he could not save himself from one or two severe wounds. Giving way before the fierce, unremitting attack of his antagonist, he came without knowing it to the edge of the well, stumbled over the raised parapet that surrounded it, and fell headlong into its depths.[1]

---

[1] A skeleton has been found in the well of the Brading Villa.

The sight of the conflict had diverted Carna's attention from the burning house. She did not wait to see its issue, but at once quitted the precincts of the villa. Some of the survivors of the garrison, the old priest and his wife, and the rest of the non-combatants, followed her. Not only did they feel that it was she who had saved them from the swords of the Saxons, but they recognized in her calmness and courage the qualities of a true leader, and were sure that they could not do better than follow her guidance. Her own plans had been formed for some time. She saw that the strength of Britain was in the great cities. If the country, disorganized as it was, was to be made capable again of order and self-defence, the impulse must come from them, the centres of its civil and religious life. Londinium, where the Count's name was well-known and respected, and where she had some connections of her own, was her destination. There she hoped to be able to do something for her people.

The first step was to leave the neighbourhood of the villa, and with the helpless companions who now, she saw, looked to her for guidance, to make her way to the north of the island, and from thence to the mainland. Making a short pause till the stragglers had come up, she addressed a few words of counsel and comfort to the fugitives.

"Dear friends," she said, "God has delivered us

from the hands of the heathen, and will bring us safe to the haven where we would be. But this is no place for us. We will go to where we may serve Him in peace and quietness."

Her clear, firm tones, which seemed inspired with all the confidence of an unfaltering faith, seemed to breathe in their turn new courage into the terrified crowd. They received them with a murmur of assent, and without an expression of fear or doubt, followed her as she led the way to the summit of the neighbouring downs.

Arrived at this spot, she paused and turned, as if to take a last look at the scenes in which her past life had been spent. The landscape lay calm and smiling about her. Every feature in it was familiar to her eyes; there was not one with which she had not some happy association. But now the sight had lost its power; her soul was occupied with more profound emotions. The home of her childhood lay beneath her feet, a blackened ruin; and there, upon the sea, could be seen flashing in the sunlight the oars of the Saxons' departing galleys.

It was a contrast full of significance, and the girl, in whose pure and enthusiastic soul there seemed to be something of a prophetic power, caught some of its meaning. That ruined house was the past, the days of the Roman domination. It had had its uses, it had done its work, but it had become corrupt and feeble, and it was passing away for ever. And the future was there, symbolized in the Saxon ships that, brightened by the sunshine, were speeding their way, instinct, as it seemed, with a vigorous and hopeful life, across the waters. That was the new power that was to shake this worn-out civilization, and raise in the course of the ages a fair fabric of its own.

For the moment the present, with all its misery and desolation, mastered the girl's spirit with an overpowering sense of loss. Thoughts of her ruined home, her helpless country, and her own personal loss, though almost unacknowledged to herself, in the final parting with the young hero of her life, came upon her with a force which broke down all her fortitude. She covered her face with her hands and wept.

Then her fortitude and her conscience reasserted themselves. "Courage, my friends," she cried, "God hath not deserted us, nor our dear country. We have sinned much, and we shall have much to bear. But He has chosen this land for a great work, and He will make all things work together for good till He has accomplished it." She was silent for a few moments. When she began to speak again, some mighty inspiration seemed to carry her beyond the present and out of herself. "Yes," she cried, "God hath great things in store for this dear

CARNA ON THE HILLSIDE.

country of ours. I see a great blackness of darkness. From many houses, great and fair, where the rulers of the land lived delicately, shall go up to heaven the smoke of a great burning, and the fields shall be untilled and desolate, and the rivers shall run red with blood. But beyond the darkness I see a light, and the light shines upon a land that is fair as the garden of the Lord; and therein I behold great cities thronged with men, and in the midst of them stately houses of God, such as have never yet been built by skill of human hand. And the people that work and worship there are not of our race, nor yet wholly strange. For the Lord shall make to Himself a people from out of them that know Him not, even from the rovers of the sea; they that pull down His Church shall build it again, and they shall carry His name to many lands, for the sea shall be covered with their ships; and they shall rule over the nations from the one end of heaven to the other."

She sank upon her knees, and remained wrapt in prayer, while the crowd stood round and watched her with awe-stricken faces. When she rose again to her feet she was calm. Resolutely she set her face from the scene of her past life, and went her way to meet the future that lay before her.

CHAPTER XXX.

AT LAST.

IT was nearly sunset on the second day of the great battle of Badon Hill.[1] The long, desperate fight was over, and the great British champion had turned back for a time the tide of Saxon invasion. The heathen dead lay, rank by rank, as they had fallen, every man in his place, in the great wedge-like formation which had resisted all the efforts of the Britons during the first day of the struggle, and had been with difficulty broken through on the second.

The King was sitting amidst a circle of his knights on the top of the hill, resting from his toils. His cross-hilted sword stood fixed in the ground before him. On one side lay his helmet, bearing for its crest a dragon wrought in gold ; on the other, his shield, on which was blazoned the figure of the Virgin.

---

[1] The battle of Badon Hill, fought in 451, seems to be a well authenticated historical fact. King Arthur defeated the Saxons after a fierce conflict which lasted for two days. Badon Hill is near Bath.

A priest approached, walking in front of a party of four who were carrying a litter, and who, at a sign from their leader, set it down before the King.

" My lord," said the priest, " I was traversing the field to see whether I could serve any of the wounded with my ministrations, when word was brought to me that a Saxon desired to talk with me. He could speak the British tongue, it was told me, a thing almost unheard of among these barbarians. I did not delay to visit the man, and finding that he desired above all things to speak to your lordship, I took it upon myself to order that he should be brought."

The wounded man raised himself with some difficulty, and by the help of one of the bearers, into a sitting posture. He was of almost gigantic proportions, and though his hair and beard were white as snow, showed little of the waste and emaciation of age.

One of the King's knights recognized him at once.

" I noted him," said he, " for a long time during the battle. He was in the front rank, and stood close to a young chief, whose guardian he seemed to be. I observed that he was content to ward off blows that were aimed at the young man, but never dealt any himself. What came to him and his charge afterwards I do not know, for the tide of battle carried me away."

" What do you want ? " said the King.

" My lord King," said the old man, speaking British fluently, though with a foreign accent, "the knight speaks true. Neither to-day, nor yesterday, nor indeed through all the years during which my people have fought with yours, have I stained my hands with British blood. Indeed for forty years I have not set foot on this island. But this year I was constrained to come, for the young Prince of my people, Logrin by name, was with the army, and his father had given him into my charge, and I could not leave him. All day, therefore, I stood by him, and warded off the blows with such strength and skill as I had, and when his death hour came, for he fell on the morning of the second day, I cared no more for my own life. So much I say that you may listen to me the more willingly, though report says of you that you are generous, not to friends only, but also to foes. But I have something to say that is of more moment. Many years ago I was a prisoner in this land, having been taken by one of the ships of Count Ælius. Many things happened to me during my sojourn here of which it does not concern me to speak, except of this. There was in the household of the Count a maiden, his daughter by adoption, but of British birth, Carna by name. She was very anxious to bring me to faith in her Master, Christ ; and I was no little moved by her words, and still more by the example of her goodness. But I loved her, and this love seemed to hinder me, for how could I tell whether it were truth itself or the love that was persuading me? And would not he be the basest of men who for love of a woman should leave the faith of his fathers? So I remained, though it was half against my own mind, in my unbelief, and when she would not take me for her husband, being unbaptized, we parted, and I saw her no more. But her words, and the memory of her, have dwelt with me unceasingly, and now that God has brought me back to this land, I desire to have that which once I refused. But tell me, my lord King, have you any knowledge of this lady Carna?"

"Yes," said the King, " I know her well, and by the ordering of God, as I do not doubt, she is in this very place this day, for she gives her whole time to ministering to such as are in trouble or sorrow. She shall be sent for forthwith, and the archbishop also, who will, if he thinks fit, administer to you the holy rite of baptism."

Cedric, for as my readers will have guessed it was he, bowed his head in assent, and after swallowing a cordial which the King's physician put to his lips, sank back upon the litter.

In about half an hour Carna appeared. She was dressed in the garb of a religious house, for she had taken the vows, and she was followed by a small company of holy women who, like her, had devoted their lives to the service of their poor and suffering brothers and sisters in Christ. Time had dealt gently with her, as he often does with gentle souls. The glossy chestnut hair of the past was changed indeed to a silvery white, and her face was wasted with fast and vigil; but her complexion was clear and delicate as of old, and her eyes as lustrous and deep.

When she saw and recognized the wounded man—for she did recognize him at once—a sweet and tender smile came over her face. Her gift of intuition seemed to tell her that her prayers were answered, and that the soul for which her supplications had gone up day by day, from youth to age, had been given to her.

" Carna," said the dying man, " God has brought me back to you after many years, and before it is too late. Your God is my God, and your country my country—but not here. Once I could not own it, fearing lest my love should be leading me into falsehood; but all things are now made clear. But, my lord King," he went on, feebly turning his head to Arthur, "bid them make haste, for I would be baptized before I die, and my time is short."

The priest had departed on another errand, and the King was perplexed. The physician whispered in his ear—

" He has not many moments to live."

" Baptize him, my lord King, yourself," said Carna; " it is lawful in case of need, and none can do it more fittingly."

" I will willingly be his sponsor," said the knight who had first spoken, " for there was never braver man wielded axe or sword."

The King dipped his hand in a golden cup that stood on the table by his chair, sprinkled the water thrice on the dying man, as he pronounced the solemn formula, and signed on his forehead the sign of the Cross. He then put the cross-shaped hilt of his sword to the lips of the newly baptized. Cedric devoutly kissed it. The next minute he was dead.

THE END.

UNWIN BROTHERS, LIMITED, PRINTERS, WOKING AND LONDON.